CONTENTS

OBITUARY FOR HOWARD GRAY

James Pattinson

CHIVERS
THORNDIKE

This Large Print edition is published by BBC Audiobooks Ltd, Bath, England and by Thorndike Press®, Waterville, Maine, USA.

Published in 2003 in the U.K. by arrangement with Robert Hale Limited.

Published in 2003 in the U.S. by arrangement with Robert Hale Limited.

U.K. Hardcover ISBN 0–7540–7388–2 (Chivers Large Print)
U.K. Softcover   ISBN 0–7540–7389–0 (Camden Large Print)
U.S. Softcover   ISBN 0–7862–5776–8 (Nightingale)

The text of this Large Print edition is unabridged.
Other aspects of the book may vary from the original edition.

Set in 16 pt. New Times Roman.

Printed in Great Britain on acid-free paper.

British Library Cataloguing in Publication Data available

ISBN 0–7862–5776–8 (lg. print : sc : alk. paper)

CHAPTER ONE

SOMETHING EXCITING

It was in the *Daily Telegraph* obituary column; a part of the paper to which Drake would not normally have given more than a cursory glance. It was the name that caught his attention on this occasion: Howard Gray.

It rang a bell, a pretty loud bell. Because he had known a Howard Gray many years ago; known him as well as you could get to know any man who was not a twin brother.

This could be a different person of course; the name was hardly uncommon. But it was the photograph that told him this was his man; a Howard Gray grown older of course—as hadn't we all—but with the same basic features that he found unmistakable.

So Howard was dead; gone to a better land or maybe a worse. Some people, if they had still been living, might have placed a small, or even a large wager on its being the latter. Always supposing that the dear departed invariably got their just deserts in the end. Which was doubtful.

Drake read on. And there was quite a lot to read; since any man who had amassed a fortune running into many millions was almost certain to have had a life that had not been

1

without its interesting aspects. Yet when he came to the end of his reading he knew that it was not all there; no, not by a long chalk. Whoever had written the obituary had either not known the half of the story or had deliberately left much of it out. He wondered who that person was.

The photograph could not have been a recent one, for it portrayed a man who was certainly little more than middle-aged. Yet Gray had been as old as he, Edgar Charles Drake, was; and when he looked in a mirror he saw the face of a man getting on for eighty; a face that time had been at work on with the inevitable and regrettable result. No more catching of the female eye for that face; those days were gone. It was sad, but the fact had to be faced. It was always old Father Time who had the last laugh.

Drake had been at school with Gray. They had been pals then, and later. It might have been the attraction of opposites, for they certainly differed from each other in almost every way. Gray was a charmer, no doubt about that: dark-haired, well-built, good-looking, with the gift of the gab and no great respect for the strict truth when it suited his purpose not to be. He could really spin a yarn.

Sometimes Drake would tax him with this. 'You're an awful liar, Howard. Have you no respect for the truth?'

Gray merely laughed. 'What is truth? It's all

2

in the mind, Eddie, all in the mind.'

Which was nonsense, of course, but not something that Drake was prepared to argue about. This was Gray, the way he was made, and you had to take him as he was, faults and all. Neither of them had been much above average as scholars, though good at games, and they had left school at a period when it was the exception rather than otherwise to proceed to university. There were not so many of them around in those days.

At a time of high unemployment they might perhaps have considered themselves fortunate to be taken on by a large insurance company and set to work in their London office. They shared modest lodgings in Canning Town and travelled to work each day on the Tube, which was not the most pleasant of journeys during the rush hour.

Gray, with his black hair and clean-cut features that a hero of the silver screen might have envied, was even more of a charmer now that he had reached maturity than he had been as a boy. He might not have been able to charm the birds out of the trees, but he could certainly work his magic on the wingless variety who tapped the keys of the typewriters in the offices of the Apex Insurance Company in Chancery Lane in the City of London.

'I don't know how you do it,' Drake said. 'You've got them eating out of your hand. What on earth do they see in you?'

Gray laughed. 'The answer to a maiden's prayer, that's what. Not jealous, are you?'

Drake repudiated the suggestion. 'Me, jealous? Perish the thought.'

But he was. A little. Or maybe rather more than a little, if the truth were told.

Not that Gray was at all selfish. He was generous enough to pass on some of his surplus to Drake. The snag in this arrangement from the recipient's point of view was that he never got the best of the bunch; and it was all too obvious that those he did get regarded him as a kind of consolation prize and only came along because Gray was in the party.

They were always short of money in those days. The Apex might have assets running into billions of pounds sterling but very little of this wealth filtered down to the employees on the lower rungs of the promotion ladder. This shortage of cash rather tended to cramp their style. After paying the rent of their lodgings and all the other expenses that had to be met there was really not a great deal left to spend on riotous living. Their leisure time was hardly packed with the mad delights of wine, women and song; and if they went to the theatre the seats were usually in the lofty regions known commonly as the Gods.

The cinema provided a brief escape from the dull realities of life, and there was always the palais de danse with the music, if not of the

4

likes of Victor Sylvester or Roy Fox, at least of some band which could bash out the rhythms that set the feet moving.

But soon they felt the urge to break free from this net that seemed to be holding them in its mesh.

'We're wasting our youth,' Gray said. 'It's all so damned humdrum. The same old routine day after day. Why don't we make a clean break? Do something exciting.'

'Like what, for example?'

Gray gave it some thought. Then: 'How about hiking round the world?'

'You're crazy,' Drake said.

'No, I'm not. Think about it. Think what an adventure it would be; always something new just round the corner. Think of the sights we'd see: the Taj Mahal, the Grand Canyon, Victoria Falls, Sydney Harbour Bridge and everything. Think of the cities we'd visit: Paris, New York, Buenos Aires, Rio de Janeiro— Doesn't it sound great? Set the blood tingling.'

'Oh, sure, it sounds fine. But it's just not on, is it?'

'Why not?'

'Well for a start, what do we do for money?'

Gray smiled. 'No problem. We work, that's what. Get jobs here and there, stick at it for a while, build up a bit of capital and then move on. Take it in easy stages, see?'

Drake stared at him. 'Are you serious about this?'

5

'Betcher life, I am. So what do you say? Are you game to take it on or are you just a lily-livered softie?'

When he put it like that there could be only one possible answer.

'I'm game,' Drake said.

*   *   *

They planned it. They planned it for days, weeks, months, all that golden summer. They bought an atlas and plotted the route. There would, of course, be parts of the journey which would entail sea voyages. Gray maintained that this was no problem.

'If we haven't got the cash for a ticket we'll just have to work our passage.'

He made it sound easy, but Drake had doubts. Surely you would need some experience to be taken on as a deckhand. But he said nothing. He was dazzled by this prospect of travelling round the world, even as Gray was, and the problem of crossing those awkward bits of water was a mere detail.

They had told their families nothing about the project. Parents could be so lacking in vision. There would be shock and horror at the very idea of chucking up a safe job at a time when there was so much unemployment and millions on the dole. It would be regarded as utter madness.

'We'll write to them when we're on our way,'

Gray said. 'It'll be *a fait accompli.* Nothing they can do about it then.'

So the planning went ahead. They bought rucksacks and calculated how much could be carried without overburdening themselves. They went into training with long walks at weekends and saved money by having fewer evenings on the town.

They had decided that early autumn might be as good a time as any to set out on their epic journey. At that time the weather would still be mild, and before winter set in they would be in the warm south—the Riviera or even the land of the Pharaohs.

'I've always wanted to see the pyramids,' Gray said. 'And the Sphinx. Eddie, my boy, we're going to have the time of our lives. It'll be goodbye to the office desk and hurrah for the great adventure.'

*   *   *

It all came to nothing, of course. The dream ended on the Third of September when Neville Chamberlain sadly informed the British people that as from five p.m. on that day they were at war with Germany.

CHAPTER TWO

HEROES

'I'm not waiting to be conscripted,' Gray said. 'I'm going to volunteer. How about you, Eddie?'

'You can count me in,' Drake said. It had not occurred to him before, but now that Howard mentioned it, it seemed the obvious thing to do.

'That other project will have to be put on hold for the present. Must get this business finished with first.'

'How long do you think it will take?'

'Oh, six months or so. Maybe a year.'

'As long as that?'

'Well, maybe not. We shall just have to wait and see. First thing is to get in on it.'

'Which lot do we join?'

Gray gave the question some thought. Then: 'Navy, I'd say. If we learn to be sailors it could come in handy afterwards. Besides, I've always had a certain hankering for a life on the ocean wave. And you've got the right name for it, haven't you? Sir Francis and all that. So how about it?'

'I've no objection.'

'Just think of it. Before long we could be on board one of those great battleships, or maybe a cruiser.'

'How about a destroyer?'

'One of those long, lean greyhounds of the sea. Yes, that would be fine.'

* * *

Their departure from the office was quite an occasion. Some of the girls shed tears, and they felt like heroes going off to fight for King and Country. They were assured that when they returned after the war, victorious of course, their jobs would be waiting for them at Apex. No one was tactless enough to mention the possibility that they might never return; and that unpleasant thought did not for a moment find houseroom in the heads of the two who were about to set off on the path of glory. They were both still young enough to feel themselves as immortal as the gods.

So they shook, as it were, the Apex dust from off their shoes and departed to do their service in some fine ship that flew the White Ensign from its jack-staff.

* * *

Six months later they were seaman-gunners on board a rusty old cargo vessel sailing in a convoy of forty merchantmen outward bound from Loch Ewe. Gone were all their dreams of serving in some fine ship of the Royal Navy, a

9

battle-wagon, a cruiser, a destroyer or even a humble corvette or minesweeper. They were naval ratings, but they were part of an organisation known as DEMS—Defensively Equipped Merchant Ships. The defensive equipment of the S.S. *Dangate* which sailed under the Red Ensign and not the White, consisted of two old Hotchkiss machine-guns mounted on the wings of the bridge for anti-aircraft work, an even older 4-inch breech-loader at the stern for use against any U-boat that might come to the surface within range, and a high-angle 12-pounder which would at a pinch serve either purpose not very well.

Neither Drake nor Gray had much faith in any of these antiquated weapons, but concluded that they were the best that were available at that early stage in the conflict.

'Better than nothing, I suppose,' Gray said.

'But not much.'

Some ships had Lewis guns, which were better. They had been trained in the use of these as well as the Marlin, which was an old American machine-gun, belt fed and liable to jam. The Hotchkiss jammed easily too; it was fed by a metal strip with the rounds clipped on the underside. When the gun fired the vibration tended to cause some of the rounds to fall out of their clips and stop the action. Nice going! Gray said that in his opinion it made little difference.

'What chance would there be of bringing

down a Dornier or a Focke-Wulf with a three-o-three bullet even if you managed to hit the bastard?'

'Spitfires and Hurricanes fire three-o-threes,' Drake said. 'Sure they do. But they fire more of them and they get closer to the target.'

*   *   *

There were two other seaman-gunners on board, and the four of them were under the command of a veteran leading seaman named Lock, who had been called up as a reservist. He had done service in naval ships and regarded his present appointment as an undeserved imposition. He was a skeleton of a man with a bald head and a habitual sour expression. To those under his command he was known as the killick, since all leading seamen in the Navy were nicknamed killicks because of the anchor on the sleeve denoting their rank.

The gunners' quarters were at the stern of the ship under the poop, close to those of the crew. The cabin they occupied was cramped, the bunks two-tiered, leaving little room for lockers and a wooden table at which they ate their meals. While the ship was at sea they could hear the beating of the propeller and the rattle of the rudder chains. There was a pervading odour of oil and paint and too many

11

unbathed bodies crammed into too small a space. There was a reek of oilskins and damp duffel coats, of stale cigarette smoke and the killick's filthy pipe in which he smoked some kind of tobacco probably known only to seafaring men. What amazed Drake was how quickly you became accustomed to such living conditions and took them in your stride.

Fortunately, neither he nor Gray was troubled with seasickness, and they ate with healthy appetites the food that was provided. The galley was amidships, and here a slob of a sea cook in blue cotton trousers and a grubby singlet plied his trade on a coal-burning stove, assisted by a skinny youngster with a perpetual cough and a dripping nose.

As Gray remarked, it was not exactly catering of the cordon bleu variety.

'Do you think they ever wash their hands?'

'I try not to let my mind dwell on things like that,' Drake said. 'It might put me off my grub.'

There were two ladders and a well-deck between the poop and the galley, and in rough weather, with the ship rolling, this stretch of steel deck was often awash. In such conditions carrying meals from one end to the other became a hazardous undertaking.

'Sometimes, Eddie old son,' Gray said, 'I wonder just why we were so eager to volunteer.'

'Because we were young and stupid, that's

12

why.'

'You could be right.'

'Anyway, would you want to be back at the office desk, bored out of your mind?'

'Since you ask,' Gray said, 'I must admit that there are odd moments when even boredom has a certain nostalgic charm about it.'

But there was no going back. Come what might, for good or bad, they were in it now.

Lock, the old killick, had a contempt for merchant ships and kept himself as much as possible aloof from the crew, though he could not avoid all contact with those who were chosen to act as auxiliaries in the 4-inch gun crew. He had to put them through the drill, which he did with no apparent enthusiasm and a gloomy expression which seemed to indicate no great faith in the adequacy of the human material he had in hand.

To the four young naval ratings he was a kind of father figure; they might make fun of him behind his back, but they had a sneaking respect for a man with so much experience of the sea.

'Has it occurred to you, Eddie,' Gray remarked, 'that he was doing his stuff on board a warship when you and I were still in swaddling-clothes?'

'I never was in swaddling-clothes,' Drake said. 'And I doubt whether you were either.'

'It was a figure of speech. He's that much

older than us. Compared to him we're mere babes in arms.'

'Some babes!' Drake said.

But he understood what Gray meant. They still had an awful lot to learn about the sea.

They were to learn some part of it just three days out from Loch Ewe. They learnt it the hard way in a late winter storm in the North Atlantic which hit the convoy like a hammer and set the ships reeling from the blow.

CHAPTER THREE

MIDDLE WATCH

Drake went on watch at midnight and he had to feel his way in the darkness. A rope had been stretched across the well-deck and it was certainly needed. The ship was rolling heavily and the deck was awash as successive waves swept over the bulwarks and flooded the scuppers. There was no light visible anywhere, but there was a faint glimmer of foam like some spectral presence moving here and there.

Drake clung to the rope and struggled forward, water swirling round his gumboots and freezing rain stinging his cheeks. The wind was making a continuous wailing sound to accompany the thunder of successive waves hitting the ship, the sinister gurgle of water

14

finding a way of escape and an intermittent rattling sound as of a prisoner in a dungeon shaking his chains.

Drake was thankful to get to the midships section and the ladder that would take him to a higher level where there was less danger of being swept away by a rush of seawater. Shortly after this he reached the small wooden enclosure on the starboard wing of the bridge where one of the Hotchkiss guns and its mounting were hidden under a canvas cover. Here, in a dripping oilskin coat and sou'wester, was the person he had come to relieve, Seaman Gunner George Pearson, a pimply-faced youngster who seemed to have a permanent chip on his shoulder.

'So,' he said, 'you're here at last. Began to think you wasn't ever coming.'

'Ah, stop moaning,' Drake said. 'I got here as fast as I could. Can't be more than a minute late at most.'

To tell the truth he could see no point in keeping these nocturnal watches at all. What possibility was there of any air attack this far out from land and in the middle of the night? He had put this question to the killick and had been informed that it was the drill.

'You're not up there just to look out for Focke-bloody-Wulfs and sodding Dormers. You're there to keep your eyes skinned for anything that comes in sight, especially U-boats.'

15

Which had a certain logic about it, Drake supposed, though hardly on a night like this when you could see nothing at all; not even the other ships of the convoy. They were out there somewhere, he supposed, but where? Suppose one of them suddenly came out of the murk and rammed the *Dangate*! Nice thought, that.

George Pearson had not hung around chatting. He had disappeared quickly and no doubt would soon be snoring in his bunk, oblivious to all the clatter and the erratic motion of the cabin. It would have taken more than that to rob a young seaman of his sleep.

Left to himself, Drake huddled in the gun box and tried to get as much shelter as possible from the the canvas cover of the gun. Time passed incredibly slowly and he had no means of judging how long he had been there, since he had no watch, and even if he had had one he would not have been able to read it in the inky darkness. He was startled when he felt a touch on his shoulder, for he had been quite unaware of anyone approaching his position on the wing of the bridge.

Then a voice said: 'Come into the wheelhouse for a spell, gunner. It's a damned hellish night.'

Drake recognized the voice. It was that of the second mate, who had the middle watch. Drake followed him to the wheelhouse and went inside, closing the door behind them. It was a relief to be out of the wind and the rain, though the storm could still be heard raging outside as if in frustration.

'This your first trip?' the second mate enquired.

He was a stocky, round-faced man named Caston; not much more than thirty years old, Drake would have reckoned. Though you could never be sure; he might have been older than he seemed. Certainly he was younger than the mate, who would relieve him for the morning watch. Mr Rayburn was a tall, lean man with a stoop and a habitual worried expression, as though he had an abiding fear of imminent disaster; and of course in the present circumstances this could hardly have been described as an unreasonable expectation.

Drake had no doubt that had this been Mr Rayburn's watch he would never have been invited to take refuge in the wheelhouse; while the third mate, Simpkin, a very young man with cherubic features and curly golden hair, would probably not have had the self-confidence to take such a liberty with normal practice.

As for Captain Flaxman, who would have been known to all the ship's company as the Old Man even if he had been as young as Simpkin, it was idle to speculate regarding what he might have done since he did not have any regular watch but might appear on the bridge at any time of the day or night. He was usually seen there for a while during the

17

morning watch, and in fine weather could often be observed pacing back and forth in company with the mate on either the port or starboard wing of the bridge, going alternately uphill or downhill as the ship rolled.

Flaxman really was an old man, comparatively speaking. Possibly he had been brought out of retirement to play his part in the war effort. His uniform too, with its tarnished gold braid, looked like something that had been stowed away in a drawer and pressed again into service like its wearer. He was a rather stout man, white-haired, and with a benign look about him; a calm man, not likely to lose his head in a crisis; a man whose easy-going manner might have been misleading, disguising the steeliness beneath the surface.

'Yes, sir,' Drake said in answer to the second mate's question. 'It is.'

'And not enjoying it very much, I should imagine, eh?'

'Not at the moment certainly. Is it often like this?'

'In the North Atlantic at this time of the year you have to expect something of the kind from time to time. It's no seaside boating lake. Still, there is one advantage, we're not likely to be bombed or torpedoed while this lasts.'

There was a faint reddish light in the wheelhouse coming from the binnacle which housed the compass. At the wheel was one of the seamen, his feet planted well apart in order to maintain his balance. He was silent, keeping an eye on the compass needle and concentrating on his job. A door, closed at present, at the back of the wheelhouse, gave access to the chartroom. Mr Caston went in there from time to time, but he did not invite Drake to accompany him. Apparently there were limits to his hospitality. And after a while he told Drake that he had better go back to his gun.

'Can't have you hanging around in here all night, can we?'

'No sir.'

So he left the wheelhouse and clawed his way back to the wing of the bridge, where he found the gun cover had come loose and was flapping madly in the wind. The wet canvas struck him in the face and it stung; but after a brief wrestling match he managed to get it under control and secured it with a length of cord. After which he resigned himself to enduring another hour or two of duty, peering into the blackness, stamping his feet in a vain endeavour to get some warmth into them and trying to avoid being flung off balance by the mad convulsions of the ship.

*   *   *

It was still dark and there seemed to no abatement of the storm when Gray came to

19

relieve him.

'Nice weather,' Gray said, and he had to shout to make himself heard. 'Anything exciting taking place?'

'Like what?'

'You tell me.'

'There's nothing to tell,' Drake said. 'And I'm not going to stand here chinwagging with you, because I've had enough of it. Good night.'

'What's good about it?' Gray said.

But he got no answer. Drake was already on his way to the creature comforts of the gunners' quarters; such as they were.

He went down the ladders backwards, holding on with both hands and planting his feet carefully on the steps. When he came to the well-deck he groped for the rope and found it. And then it was the struggle again in the reverse direction, with the bulwark dipping as the vessel rolled, and the sea spilling over and threatening to sweep him off his feet and maybe slam him against the hatch coamings for good measure.

But he made it to the poop and the cabin where a dim blue electric bulb provided a subdued illumination. He got himself out of his oilskins and duffel coat and kicked off his gumboots while the cabin tilted first one way and then another as if in an attempt to frustrate his efforts. The noise, which never ceased for a moment, was like an echo of that

20

outside, but it failed to disturb the gunners sleeping in their bunks as soundly as if they had been in the softest of beds in a quiet room ashore.

He sat down at the table, which was screwed to the deck and had a fiddle all round the edge to prevent plates and dishes sliding off, and lit a cigarette and drew smoke into his lungs. Now and then, as the stern of the ship lifted, the propeller would break the surface and send an extra shudder through the cabin, but it failed to awaken the sleepers or even disturb their slumbers. The *Dangate* was carrying no cargo on this outward voyage and only a little ballast, with the result that she rode high in the water and was all the more prone to rolling heavily as well as pitching and tossing.

Drake's cigarette was a Capstan taken from a round tin of fifty which he had bought from the chief steward, a fleshy man with moist lips and a watery eye, as well as a reputed tendency to homosexuality. One of his duties was to dole out dry rations to the gunners and crew. These comprised bread, butter, cheese, tea, coffee, sugar and condensed milk. The milk never lasted a full week because most of the gunners appeared to have a taste for strong syrupy tea. But Gray could always persuade the steward to part with a few extra tins. He just turned on the charm, as he knew so well how to do.

The killick was a trifle contemptuous of this,

though he was not above taking a share of the extra ration.

'Just don't let him catch you bending, that's all,' he said.

Drake took a last pull at his cigarette, stubbed it out in a tin lid that served as an ashtray and climbed into his bunk without bothering to undress further. For a minute or two he lay awake listening to all the creaking and rattling, and thankful that there was a board to prevent him from rolling out of his nest. As he lay there it occurred to him to wonder whether by any chance this rusty old wanderer of the high seas might break up and sink without any help from the enemy. For surely it was not unheard of even in these days for ships to founder under the battering of a storm and go to the bottom of the ocean with all hands. For what hope would there have been of launching a lifeboat in such conditions? None at all, to his way of thinking.

But he did not brood on this subject for long, because sleep came quickly to blot out all consciousness of wave and wind, of screeching metal and creaking timber. If he slept like a log it could only have been a log that was constantly being made to imitate the action of a seesaw while simultaneously being rolled from side to side.

Seaman Gunner Edgar Drake was oblivious of this. He slept on in his narrow bunk and dreamed of other things.

CHAPTER FOUR

REAL SEAMEN

He was awakened by a different kind of shaking from that which was being inflicted on him by the elements. The storm appeared to have abated very little during his brief spell of sleep, but it was a hand on his shoulder roughly shaking it and a voice in his ear that brought him to a state of reluctant wakefulness.

'Come on, you dozy bastard. Show a leg, show a leg.'

The voice was that of Leading Seaman Walter Lock and it was his hand that was grasping Drake's shoulder in a none too gentle grip. For an instant the thought sprang into Drake's mind that some disaster had occurred and that he ought to be getting his life-jacket on as quickly as possible. This idea was banished by the killick's next words.

'It's breakfast time, son, and it's your turn to fetch it.'

There was no arguing with that. Drake would have been happy to remain in the bunk and go back to sleep; you never seemed to have enough of it at sea. But he knew that he would not be allowed to do so; in this little group to which he now belonged the word of

23

one gnarled old leading seaman was law.

Drake, obedient to the law, eased himself out of the bunk, pulled on the gumboots which he had so recently discarded and with some difficulty because of the continuing erratic behaviour of the cabin, arrayed himself once again in duffel coat and oilskins.

'Now mind how you go,' Lock said. 'Don't go spilling our grub all over the deck.'

'I'll do my best,' Drake promised.

'You'd better, son, you'd better.'

Out on the open deck conditions seemed to have altered little since he had come off watch, though there was some faint indication that day might be breaking. Vague shapes were looming out of the murk, and the rain had eased.

Drake was carrying a nest of three white enamel food containers which fitted, one above another with a lid on top, into a metal carrier. Thus he now had only one free hand with which to cling to rope or rail. But he was learning a trick or two and knew when to move forward and when simply to cling on for dear life. He even experienced a certain satisfaction in winning this battle with the elements.

When he reached the galley he found the cook in a vile mood. He could hardly be blamed for this. The galley was in a mess, with wet cinders and coal-dust underfoot and the stove, on which it was his task to prepare meals for the whole ship's company, performing a kind of jig as the vessel rolled and plunged. It amazed Drake that he could manage at all in such conditions. There were saucepans on the stove, and these would certainly have been sliding off if it had not been for iron bars holding them in place.

The second cook, who was little more than a galley boy, was bearing the brunt of the cook's ill temper. It seemed he could do nothing to the satisfaction of his superior, and he was so repeatedly sworn at and verbally assaulted that he was close to tears.

There was a half-door to the galley with a ledge on the inner side. Drake parked his containers on the ledge and said: 'Gunners.'

The cook, who was busy at the stove, turned his head and stared at him in not a very friendly manner. Drake would not have been surprised if the man had sworn at him too, but maybe he thought it best not to antagonize a naval rating. Instead he gave a nod to his assistant, who took the containers and loaded them with breakfasts for five.

'You took your time,' Lock said when Drake had clawed his way back to the gunners' quarters. 'What'd you do? Take a rest on the way?'

Drake gathered that this was the killick having his little joke, so he took no notice. Some of the warmth had gone out of the food during its journey, but this had no effect on the appetites of those who sat down to eat it. And it had to be admitted that the cook had not done at all badly in the circumstances. There was porridge, fried sausage, bacon and eggs, and for those who liked it, curry and rice. It was odd, Drake reflected, that curry and rice turned up every day for breakfast and nobody ever ate it. It just went overboard with the rest of the gash. He hoped the fish liked curry.

One of the ratings started moaning about the weather. 'How long is it going to last like this. I'm fair sick of it.'

'Sick of it!' Lock said. 'What's wrong with you? You don't know when you're well off, my lad. You oughter see what it's like in one of them little corvettes. Compared with them, you're on easy street, and don't you forget it.'

Drake reflected that if this was easy street he hated to think what life on board a corvette was like. It must be sheer hell.

*   *   *

During the course of the day the storm gradually abated. The rain stopped and the wind became less boisterous, but it was still bitterly cold. By midday the clouds had broken up to allow some weak sunlight to peep through; though this gave little warmth.

Drake, rather to his surprise, saw that the convoy seemed to be intact. He counted the ships and by his reckoning they were all there, with the destroyers in the escort dashing here and there like collie dogs rounding up a flock of sheep.

Still there had been no sign of the enemy, above or beneath the surface. They had seen no long-range convoy raider in the sky, and though a few depth charges had been dropped by the warships these seemed to have been more of a precautionary measure than anything else.

'Asdic operators thought they got an echo,' Lock said. 'Maybe they sank a whale.'

It was his opinion that the convoy would get through without trouble. 'The ships are all empty, ain't they? Jerry won't bother with them. It's the eastbound convoys that get the hammer.'

Drake wondered whether he had any evidence to support this statement. He had his doubts. A ship was a ship, with cargo or without, and thus a valuable target. Surely the U-boats would not let a convoy pass simply because it was outward bound. You could be pretty sure of that.

But he did not argue. Who was he to question the wisdom of a veteran like Walter Lock, with the anchor on his sleeve and his gunlayer's badge? He just hoped the man would be correct in his prognostication.

And in the event he was.

*　　*　　*

27

The convoy dispersed long before land was in sight, the merchant ships going their various ways and the escort vessels leaving them to their own devices.

To Leading Seaman Lock's disgust the S.S. *Dangate* was heading for Halifax, Nova Scotia. 'That's a dead-and-alive place if ever there was one.'

'In what way?' Drake asked.

'Well, for a start, it's dry.'

'How do you mean—dry?'

'I mean like the States used to be.'

'Are you saying they've got prohibition?'

'Sort of. You won't find any pubs there. Only place you can buy a bottle of the hard stuff is at a licensed liquor store and then it's rationed. They give you a temporary liquor permit. It's all to do with the Nova Scotia liquor control act or some such.'

'How about the people who live in the place?'

'Don't ask me. Maybe they have permanent liquor permits. I don't know.'

'Well, this way they don't get a lot of drunken sailors wrecking the place. So maybe they're not so stupid at that.'

*   *   *

Drake went ashore with Gray and came to the conclusion that Lock had been doing Halifax an injustice when he had called it a dead-and-

28

alive place. There were plenty of shops and restaurants and cinemas; and there were probably whorehouses as well if you knew where to look for them.

'Well,' Gray said, 'we've done our first crossing of the Atlantic, so I suppose we're entitled to call ourselves real seamen now, wouldn't you say?'

'We've still got a lot to learn.'

'Oh, sure we have. But we've had a real taste of what the Atlantic can do. I don't imagine it can get much worse than that.'

'We could be torpedoed,' Drake said.

'I don't believe it. We're going to be the lucky ones. I feel it in my bones.'

'I guess nearly everybody feels like that. We all think we're immortal and that anybody else may get it in the neck but not us. And we could be wrong, you know; we could be so very wrong.'

'Cheerful bugger, aren't you?' Gray said.

The S.S. *Dangate* remained several days in dock, taking on board a mixed cargo, chiefly of foodstuffs—cans and cans of meat products, beans, peas, fruit, condensed milk, fish—all packed in crates and lowered into the holds in rope slings. This kind of activity was all new to Drake and he watched with interest the stevedores down in the bowels of the ship handling the slings as they came down, guiding them to the correct positions and then unloading them. The men looked like

29

lumberjacks; most of them were dressed in blue jeans and plaid jackets with peaked leather caps on their heads. He noticed that they all wore coarse leather gloves and they were using cargo hooks to aid them in handling the crates.

He asked Lock whether British dockers wore gloves, and the killick shook his head.

'They'd think it was cissie.'

The Canadians did not look like cissies to Drake. Far from it. And he thought they were pretty smart to protect their hands. The job looked fairly hazardous anyway; things could fall on you down there. Still, they would not be going with the cargo, so they would not be exposed to that greater danger which was waiting for the ship many miles from the rocky shores of Nova Scotia.

CHAPTER FIVE

DANGEROUS MOONLIGHT

It happened when they were ten days out from Halifax. A convoy of thirty merchant ships had gathered for the eastward voyage, all fully laden and most of them having come up from the south. Four of them were tankers from the Gulf with their deadly cargoes of high octane petrol.

'Wouldn't want to be on one of them,' Lock said. 'One hit and up she goes like a bloody torch. Not nice being burnt alive, not nice at all.'

Drake could agree with that. In the bad old days witches and heretics were burnt at the stake with faggots. There had been progress since then. Now the fuel was liquid.

They had been lucky with the weather for those early days of the voyage, and the convoy had forged ahead at a steady seven knots with no stragglers to make things difficult for the escort. Even the *Dangate*, with her elderly reciprocating engine, was managing to keep her station fairly well at number three in the outer starboard column, though now and then she was pouring out more smoke than was really acceptable. Smoke could be seen from a long distance and reveal the position of the convoy to enemy eyes.

Drake and Gray were now thoroughly accustomed to the routine of life on board: the watch-keeping, the servicing of the weapons, the washing of clothes, the fetching of meals, the cleaning of quarters for the captain's weekly inspection . . .

It seemed remarkable to Drake that a handful of men, so different from one another in character, class and upbringing, should yet exist so harmoniously in the cramped conditions of the gunner's cabin. There was very little bickering, and even the snarling of

31

the old killick seemed to be accepted more with amusement than resentment.

We're all in the same boat, he thought. Which was literally as well as figuratively true. They faced the same dangers, the same discomforts, and they had better make the best of things.

*   *   *

There was a full moon when he went on watch and the sea was as calm as it was ever likely to be in those waters. The moonlight silvered the ripples, and the dark shapes of the vessels ahead and astern and to port seemed utterly motionless, each fixed in its own position in the vast rectangle of the convoy like toys stuck to a board. He could hear the thumping of the engine and feel the vibration that ran through the ship, while the acrid fumes coming back from the smokestack caught in his throat. There was a slicing of water at the bows, and astern there stretched a ghostly pathway of pale churned-up ocean through which the blades of the propeller had carved a way.

It was all so calm, so apparently peaceful; it was hard to imagine that somewhere ahead the killers might be waiting, submerged or on the surface; the wolves preparing to attack. And that very moonlight which made so magical a picture of the scene might in fact be the most treacherous of seeming friends. Better no doubt for safety's sake a pitch-black night and a stormy sea.

This thought had barely come into his mind when the first ship was hit. It was one of the tankers near the head of the convoy, and, as the killick had said, it went up like a torch.

'Oh, Christ!' he muttered. 'This is it.'

This was the real thing. You had thought about it time and again, imagining the way it would be and how you would react to it. You were prepared for it and yet totally unprepared. There was no way of anticipating the shock, the churning of the bowels, the dread.

'Oh, Jesus Christ Almighty!'

The alarm-bells were ringing now. The sleepers were waking. They were pulling on boots and duffel coats and life-jackets, cursing, running to their action stations. The Old Man would be on the bridge now. Maybe he had been there already, knowing the possibility, the probability even, of what might happen on a night like this, knowing how dangerous the moonlight could be.

Drake became aware of Gray's presence beside him.

'Here we go then,' Gray said. He sounded calm, no hint of panic in his voice. 'That really is some fire.'

The tanker was burning fiercely. It appeared to be moving astern, but this was an illusion; it was in fact the other ships overtaking it as it lost way. Those behind were giving it a wide berth as they passed it, some on one side, some on the other.

The *Dangate* was a considerable distance away from the burning tanker when she overtook it, but there was a light breeze blowing the flames in their direction and they could feel the heat. They could see no lifeboats; there would have been no time to launch any; but there was a raft with some men clinging to it. There were some heads visible in the water, but there was a fire on the surface and it was spreading towards them.

'Poor devils,' Gray muttered. 'They've had it. They didn't stand a chance.'

And he and Drake could only stand and watch. There was nothing they could do to help the doomed men. The S.S. *Dangate* forged ahead and left the stricken tanker to its fate.

* * *

Two more ships were picked off during the night. Daylight came and the convoy closed its gaps and altered course, signals fluttering from the halyards of the commodore's ship. Some time later the signal was given to alter course again in the opposite direction. It was the zigzagging manoeuvre designed to fox the U-boats. Not all ship's captains favoured this practice; they would have preferred to forge

34

straight ahead and avoid lengthening the voyage in this way, of the efficacy of which they were doubtful to say the least.

It was an edgy time on board the *Dangate*. A sharp lookout was kept from various parts of the ship, everyone scanning the water for the slightest glimpse of a periscope or conning-tower. Destroyers and corvettes darted here and there, while now and then the hull of the ship reverberated to the shock waves of depth-charges.

'Do you think they're hitting anything?' Drake asked.

He was putting the question to Leading Seaman Lock who was standing beside him on the poop, where the massive barrel of the 4-inch gun pointed over the stern like a giant admonishing finger.

Lock answered morosely that he doubted it. 'They're just trying to scare the buggers away. Some hope.'

'Maybe we've shaken them off.'

'Not a chance. Look, son, we're doing seven knots and zigzagging. Right?'

'Right.'

'So how do you shake off sodding U-boats as can do fifteen on the surface?'

'But if they came to the surface in daylight the escort would sink them with gunfire, wouldn't they?'

'If they could see them, yes. But suppose they keep out of sight, make a detour and forge ahead. Then lay in wait for us. Hit us again tonight.'

'You say them. So you think there's more than one?'

'Betcher life there is. They hunt in packs just like real wolves. And somehow they seem to know just where we are. Well of course they don't need no telling where we're heading. There's only one way for us to go.'

'But the Atlantic's a big stretch of water. They can't cover it all.'

'True. But there's codes, ain't there? Maybe they've got ways of breaking our codes and intercepting signals that's supposed to be secret. They're clever bastards. Maybe they get told just where we are. By the wireless, see? Then they home in on us and give us a hard time. Tell you what, son, there's lots of places I'd rather be right now than this here. And that's a fact.'

It occurred to Drake that if he had been looking for a bit of cheer from the killick he had come to the wrong shop. Lock was obviously a realist and he knew the score.

*   *   *

Later he told Gray what Lock had said.

'You shouldn't listen to him,' Gray said. 'Just because he served his time in the Navy doesn't mean he knows everything about modern submarine warfare.'

'So you think he's wrong?'

Gray shook his head and gave a grin. 'No, Eddie boy,' he said. 'I think he's dead right. Unfortunately.'

CHAPTER SIX

A NIGHT OF IT

There was a moon again that night. The wind had shifted direction a little but it was still no more than a light breeze. It was cold nevertheless and seemed to have a way of finding chinks in even the thickest clothing. Drake could not help shivering, and he could not be sure how much this was due to the wind and how much to a feeling of nervousness as he stood his watch.

It was eerie; all those dark, silent ships bathed in the silver moonlight. He tried to imagine the men in them, all waiting as he was for the hammer blow that might for some of them be the end of it all; all hopes, fears, delights, ambitions, passions; all love, all hate, all desire. And then what? An after-life or utter darkness and oblivion? Who could tell? For who had ever returned to tell the tale?

He thought of the vast depths of ocean beneath the ships. He pictured his body sliding down into those unimaginable depths where

37

strange creatures lived and moved and had their being; and he knew that all that kept him from this dreadful journey was the buoyancy of the air trapped within the steel walls of the ship.

He tried to cast all thoughts of this sort out of his mind, but they had a way of coming back. He flapped his arms and stamped his feet to bring some warmth into his body, and he was still doing this when the torpedo found its mark and it was the end for the S.S. *Dangate*.

The torpedo struck just abaft the bridge. It went through the old steel-plates that rivetters years ago in some Tyneside shipyard had fixed in place and it exploded in number three hold. It sent the hatch-boards flying like rockets and played havoc with the crates of food that the stevedores in Halifax had so recently stowed. Seawater gushed in and the ship began to go down by the stern.

His memory of what happened after that was always confused; there was no order in it. There was the alarm, the stopping of the engine, the rush to boat stations and finally the signal to abandon ship. Perhaps there was some panic, but he did not notice it. Perhaps he was too absorbed in what he himself had to do.

The boat to which he had been assigned was on the port side. It was slung on old-fashioned gooseneck davits, but it had been swung outboard as soon as the ship left port and was secured by ropes to a horizontal padded spar. To launch the boat it was necessary only to release these ropes and lower it by means of the falls which ran through pulley-blocks on the davits.

In theory this sounded perfectly simple and straightforward. Drake had taken part in the exercise in port and with two or three men handling each fall the boat had been lowered without a hitch. With the ship holed below the waterline and going down by the stern the whole business became much more complicated, especially in the excitement of the moment and with some hands missing, perhaps trapped down aft by the damage to the deck that the explosion had caused.

Drake was relieved to discover that Gray was there. Their boat was under the command of Mr Rayburn, the mate, who was trying to call the roll but was handicapped by the poor light. However, he seemed to have a good memory and appeared to reel off the names by heart. Not everyone was there but it was imperative to get the boat lowered without delay and he gave the order to do so.

By now the deck was at an angle and the slope was steadily increasing, so that it was almost impossible for the men handling the falls to keep the boat level. It tilted as it went down and those who were already in it were thrown off balance. One man uttered a sharp cry of pain and it was discovered later that his right leg had been broken when it was trapped under one of the thwarts as he was flung forward.

Mr Rayburn snarled at the men on the falls to level the boat, but it still hit the water stern first and shipped several gallons before it levelled.

'Now the rest of you! Look sharp!'

They needed no urging. Drake reached out to one of the ropes dangling from the davits and slid down it to the boat, landing on one of the thwarts. Two men had already picked up oars and were trying to keep the boat from smashing against the ship's side. When you got down to that level the sea was far less placid than it had appeared from the deck of the ship. Two other men were unhooking the pulley-blocks at each end of the boat.

Mr Rayburn was the last to join them. By this time the sea had engulfed the after well-deck, and as the stern sank the bows began to lift. It could not be long before the vessel sank and it was imperative to get away before she did.

'Now you men,' Mr Rayburn snapped. 'Heave us off.'

The men obeyed at once. They thrust with the oars against the *Dangate's* side and opened up a gap between boat and ship. Other men picked up oars and began to row. Slowly the gap widened.

It was only now that Drake could turn his attention to the rest of the convoy and he saw that a long way off, near the head of the port column, another ship had been hit and a fire had broken out, though it was not one of the tankers. Suddenly it exploded; it had probably been carrying ammunition, and the sound came to them like a crack of thunder.

'Boy, oh boy!' Gray said. 'Aren't we just having a night of it!'

And it was not over yet. At that moment they became aware of a new danger. Ships astern of the *Dangate* were now overtaking the sinking vessel and the first of these was taking avoiding action. It was coming up on the port side, which was just where the two lifeboats that had got away were now situated.

Mr Rayburn was quickly aware of the danger of being run down and gave brisk orders to the men at the oars.

'Pull now! Pull!'

He himself was in the sternsheets with a hand on the tiller, and he was steering the boat away from the path of the approaching ship. They managed it by the smallest of margins; the boat was thrown about in the wash as the vessel, a big freighter with tanks on deck, went by. It was a close call; far too close for comfort.

They had been so engaged in looking to their own salvation that they had failed to notice what was happening to the other lifeboat that had been lowered on the port

41

side. Now they became aware that this boat had been hit and overturned by the bows of the passing ship. All the men who had been in it had been thrown into the churned-up water.

Mr Rayburn, observing what had happened, steered his own boat towards the floundering men, some of whom were wearing life-jackets and some not. Soon they were being hauled out of the water, drenched and shivering. But now the rescuing boat was so overcrowded it was difficult to move in it. The men at the oars had stopped rowing and the boat was simply allowed to drift.

It was discovered then that Captain Flaxman was not one of the rescued men.

Mr Rayburn questioned them. 'He was with you?'

Yes, they were sure of that. He had been the last to lower himself into the boat. So where was he now?

A cloud had drifted across the face of the moon and visibility was poor. A dark shape not far away was the overturned lifeboat, keel upward but still afloat. Was it possible that the captain had been trapped underneath it? It seemed a possibility. It could have been that he had received a blow on the head when the freighter struck the boat, knocking him unconscious. Only one thing was certain: he had gone and they would not find him now.

The sinking ship had been almost forgotten during this spell of activity. It had drifted away from them. Now someone gave a cry:

'She's gone!'

It was true. The black shape that had been the S.S. *Dangate,* just visible in the faint moonlight, had vanished. The last part of her to be seen had been the bows, jutting like a rock above the water. Now that too had disappeared.

It was an odd feeling, Drake thought, knowing that what had been your home had gone, that it was now sinking deeper and deeper to the ocean floor whose distance away from you could be measured, not just in feet or fathoms, but in miles. How long would it take for a ship to make that last journey? How long for a human body?

The boat with its freight of survivors rose and fell like a piece of flotsam. No one in that crowded space made any attempt to row, for what would have been the purpose? Gradually the convoy moved away from them and they were left behind as though no longer belonging to that community, no longer of any importance in the overall scheme of things.

Those who had been in the water were soaked to the skin and chilled to the bone. One of them was the second cook; he was shivering and his teeth were chattering. One of the other men put an arm round his shoulders and spoke some words of comfort which Drake could not catch. He was surprised to see that this other man was in fact the cook, who had never before appeared to have a kind word for his young assistant. Perhaps it took a situation like this to bring out the latent humanity in him.

It was about half an hour later when a red glow appeared on the horizon away to the east. No one believed that it was the dawn breaking.

'Another bloody tanker's copped it,' one of the seamen remarked.

Nobody contradicted him. They all knew he had to be right. What else could it be?

*   *   *

When the real dawn came they were alone. As the boat rose on the crest of a wave they scanned the wide circle of ocean that surrounded their puny craft and could see no sign of a ship. One had the feeling of having been abandoned, forgotten, as though they were of no more value and could be written off.

Nobody said much. What was there to say? They all knew the score, and it was not a score that gave much comfort to anyone.

After a while the mate gave orders to hoist a sail. So they set up a spar and rigged the canvas. Nobody believed that this was going to carry them over a thousand or more miles of sea to the nearest land, but that was not the purpose. A sail would be more easily spotted than a boat low in the water. Always supposing there was anyone in range to spot it.

Which, Drake thought gloomily, was doubtful, to say the least.

*   *   *

He was wrong. The destroyer found them soon after midday. It came from the south, fast; and when they saw it they gave a ragged cheer and waved their arms like madmen.

The destroyer hove to a few yards off, and some ratings dropped a scrambling-net over the side. They rowed those last yards to close the gap and climbed the scrambling-net; and as soon as they were all aboard the destroyer moved away quickly, because it was no place to be waiting as a sitting target for any stray U-boat that might come along.

It occurred to Drake then that though he and Gray had been in the Royal Navy for eight months or more, this was the first time that either of them had set foot on the deck of a man-of-war.

He remarked on this curious fact to Gray, and Gray said that if it never happened again in similar circumstances it would be soon enough for him.

Drake found himself unable to disagree with that.

CHAPTER SEVEN

A PERFECT DAY

They spent their two weeks of survivor's leave in London.

Most people went home on leave. They were not like most people. Gray's father, who had a not very elevated position in the Foreign Office, had for some reason or other been posted to India and had taken his wife with him. So Gray had no home to go to; the sub-continent being rather too far away.

Drake was little better off in this respect, since his parents had split up and gone their separate ways with new partners. He had no desire to plant himself on either of these households and had not even bothered to acquaint either parent with his recent experiences. He had never enjoyed much affection from his father or mother. He was an only child, and he had felt from an early age that he had been an unwanted addition to a partnership that was gradually breaking down. The wonder, to his way of thinking, was that it had lasted as long as it had.

So when Gray suggested that they should spend their leave together in the capital city he was all in favour of the idea.

And so it was settled. They managed to find

accommodation at a YMCA hostel, which was a lot cheaper than any hotel would have been, and in the event they were to need it for only one night anyway.

*   *   *

It was Gray's suggestion on their first morning in these well-remembered surroundings that they should pay a call on their old workplace, the offices of Apex Insurance. Drake suspected that he wanted to show himself off in his naval uniform and maybe tell the tale of the sinking of the S.S. *Dangate.* And to tell the truth he himself was not averse to something of the kind as well. They had had a bit of a hero's send-off on their departure; now they felt that they were returning as real heroes and revelling in the experience.

So they went along to the Apex building, and their reception was all that could have been hoped for, especially among the girls. As Gray remarked later, it was almost worth while going through the nasty part in order to enjoy the nice part later.

And it did not end there. Gray's charm seemed to be as powerful as ever; and maybe more so in his sailor's gear. The result was that two of the most attractive of the girls were persuaded without much difficulty to meet the two heroes when they finished work for an evening on the town.

Their names were Penny Rawlings and Jillian Brown. Penny was a blonde, tall and slender, and it almost went without saying that she would be Gray's partner. Jillian was a brunette and not so eye-catching as the other girl. Drake was not sure whether she would have preferred to be with Gray and only took him as second best because she knew she could not compete with the blonde, but she seemed happy enough to accept the situation as it was; so maybe she would have picked him anyway.

He, for his part, was happy enough with the arrangement. He liked brunettes; especially those as pretty as this one. She had a slightly turned-up nose and the most attractive eyes, set rather widely apart. It was the eyes that really caught him; though the whole ensemble was just right as far as he was concerned. And that included the voice. Too often, in his experience, the voice could ruin everything. But not in this case.

He could not remember having seen her during his time at Apex—and he surely would have remembered. So perhaps she had joined the company after he and Gray had left. Somebody had to do their jobs while they were away.

She told him when he asked that this was indeed the case. She had been with Apex for only six months. She also said that she did not expect to be there for very long anyway.

'How come?' Drake asked.

'Oh, I expect I'll join one of the services and do my duty for King and Country. Maybe the WAAF.'

'You'd like that?'

'It'd be more interesting, wouldn't it?'

He pictured her in uniform and thought it would suit her very well. But of course she would have looked good in anything. Or nothing at all. Now there was a thought!

*   *   *

That first evening they finished up in a bar in the West End; and they had all had rather a lot to drink when the girls said it was time they were going home. Which apparently was a flat they shared in East Finchley; a place Drake had never been to.

'We'll go with you,' Gray said.

They wouldn't hear of it.

'It's a long way. And then you'd have that journey back to the YMCA hostel you're staying at.'

'No matter,' Gray said. 'It isn't safe for two young ladies like you to travel around unescorted at this time of night. In the blackout and all. We've got to see you safely home. What do you say, Eddie?'

'Sure thing,' Drake said. He was not going to argue with Gray on a point like this.

So the girls gave in, as maybe they had

intended to do all along, and they found their way to the Leicester Square Underground station and boarded a train on the Northern Line. It was quite a long journey to East Finchley, and when they got there they had a ten-minute walk to the flat, which was on the first floor of a rather old building that had once been a single house.

'Well, now you're here,' Penny said, 'you may as well come up and see what kind of pigsty we live in.'

So they all went up a broad flight of stairs, and Penny produced a key and unlocked a door and led the way in. There were two bedrooms and a sitting-room, a bathroom and a small kitchen. The blackout blinds were already in place, so the girls must have seen to that before leaving in the morning. It was if they had anticipated having the evening out.

'So what do you think of it?' Penny said.

Gray said he thought it was very nice; which was something of an exaggeration. It was probably let furnished, and the furniture looked as if it had seen a lot of use and even misuse. There were two armchairs and a sofa, the upholstery threadbare in places, and a couple of leatherette pouffes and a three-legged stool. The carpet was pretty worn, and there was a fireplace with a gas heater standing in the hearth. On the mantelpiece were a lot of knick-knacks, a tin clock that made a loud ticking noise and wads of picture-postcards. The rest of the furniture comprised a bureau, a small table and an Ekco wireless set on a stand.

It was rather chilly in the room, until Jillian switched the heater on and lit the gas. Then it began to warm up.

They all sat around for a while, just talking. Then Penny said there was a bottle of South African sherry that had never been opened and was being saved for a special occasion. Jillian said that for her money this was certainly a special occasion. So the bottle was opened and it was not long before it was empty.

Then Penny said: 'Look, it's awfully late for you two sailor-boys to go back to that hostel where you're lodging, so why don't you stay here? One of you could sleep on the sofa, and we could make another bed with the two armchairs pushed together. So what do you say? Is it a go?'

Gray said he thought it sounded like an excellent idea, and Drake said he thought so too.

'So that's settled,' Penny said.

Then, after they'd talked some more she said she'd just remembered there was a half-bottle of brandy they were keeping for a rainy day, so how about it?

Gray said it looked very much like rain to him, though how he could tell when they were sitting in a room with the blackout curtains in place, Drake failed to see.

Anyway, the brandy bottle was opened, and before long that too was empty and they were all more than a little under the influence.

And then Penny said: 'I've been thinking. There's two bedrooms and there's two double-beds, so why in hell do we need to bother with the sofa and armchairs when there's only the four of us anyway? Will somebody tell me that?'

Nobody seemed inclined to tell her that; so it seemed as if everyone was in favour. Drake caught what looked very much like a wink from Gray, and he had a shrewd idea that this was the kind of outcome he had had in mind all along.

And if the truth had to be told, something of the sort had been in his mind also.

It seemed like the end of a perfect day.

CHAPTER EIGHT

PROMISES

He had a bad dream that night. He dreamed that he was drowning. He was struggling for his life in a turbulent sea because the ship that he had been in had been sunk by a torpedo. It was a relief to wake up to find himself in bed with the girl beside him. She was asleep, and he did not wake her. And very soon he himself went to sleep again and had no more nightmares.

*   *   *

When he woke again it was daylight and he was alone in the bed. He got up then and dressed and found Penny and Jillian in the kitchen.

'My God!' Penny said. 'You look terrible.' And she laughed.

The fact was that he was not feeling quite at the peak; he had a slight headache and a dry mouth. It was not the father and mother of all hangovers, but it was in that line of business.

'Well,' he said, 'you two look fine. So maybe you weren't drinking as much as I thought you were last night.'

'Maybe we weren't.'

'Did you sleep well?'

'When we were allowed to,' she said. And laughed again. The other girl just smiled.

'We've had breakfast,' Penny said. 'In a minute or two we'll be off to work. We were going to leave a note if you hadn't woken up. We didn't want to disturb you.'

'Some of us have to work for a living,' Jillian said. 'You'll have to get your own breakfast. There's not a lot, I'm afraid. There's a war on, you know.'

'But we can't eat your grub,' Drake said.

'That wouldn't be fair.'

'Oh, don't worry. We'll make it up off your ration cards. I suppose you've got something of the sort for your leave?'

'Yes, but—'

'So that's all right then,' Penny said. 'And we'll see you later. Same place?'

It seemed to Drake that she was taking a lot for granted. He tried to remember just what they had talked about the previous evening. A great number of things, no doubt.

'Am I getting this right?' he said. 'It seems to me you're implying that Howard and I are staying here.'

'Well of course you are, aren't you? I thought that was settled. Howard said—'

He got it then. Gray had used his charm and fixed matters for their undoubted benefit.

'What did he say?'

'Well, he said a lot of things. Anyway, you don't really want to go back to that lousy hostel, do you?'

And of course he did not. He was not that much of an idiot. But he would have to have a talk with Howard.

*   *   *

Gray was still sound asleep when the girls left on their way to work.

'You can give the place a tidy up,' Penny said as she entrusted the key to Drake. 'Being

54

sailors, you must be used to that sort of thing.'

Drake promised they would do their best.

*   *   *

Left on his own, his first act was to rouse Gray, who was not greatly pleased to be awakened.

Drake said to Gray what Penny had said to him. 'You look terrible.'

'I feel terrible. Where is everybody?'

'If you are referring to the legal tenants of this flat, they've gone to work. And what precisely did you say to Penny last night? Seems to me you arranged for us to spend our leave here. Is that correct?'

Gray combed his tousled hair with his fingers. 'Told you that, did she?'

'As good as.'

'Then it must be true.'

'You've got a nerve.'

'True, old boy, very true. And aren't you just glad I have?'

Drake did not trouble to deny it. He just said: 'Let's have some breakfast.'

*   *   *

The meal consisted largely of dry toast and strong coffee, as well as a few aspirins from the first-aid cabinet in the bathroom.

They both felt better after that, and they washed up and tidied the place a bit, as Drake had been instructed. Then they walked to the Tube station and travelled to Charing Cross, which appeared to be the nearest stop to the YMCA hostel. There they paid what they owed, picked up their kit and did the return journey to East Finchley.

*   *   *

They had not been able to shave until then, so they did so at once.

'I don't think we look quite so terrible now,' Drake said. He was feeling a great deal better than he had earlier. 'So what's next on the agenda?'

The rest of the day stretched before them, and there were no duties to perform, no watches to keep, and the evening to look forward to; the evening and the night, and more evenings and more nights ahead. They sat in the armchairs and smoked cigarettes and dozed off now and then. It was sheer bliss.

'Eddie, my boy,' Gray said, 'we've fallen on our feet. We're in clover.'

Drake tried not to think of the ephemeral nature of this happy state of affairs. Yet he knew it could not last; that it was merely an interlude, all too brief; and that when it was over it would be back to the convoys, the wretched quarters, the storms and the U-boats. Always at the back of the mind was that dark shadow which could not be entirely

56

banished in the enjoyment of the moment.

*　　*　　*

Later they went back to the West End. They found a services canteen where they were able to get a meal, and they had a couple of beers at a public house. After which they wandered aimlessly around, just killing time. There were men and women in uniform everywhere, sandbags piled in front of every important building and anti-aircaft guns in the parks. But this was a time of waiting for London and the onslaught had yet to come.

*　　*　　*

They met the girls at the same rendezvous and spent another evening on the town before returning to that love-nest in East Finchley. And so it went on from day to day. They would go to cinemas, a theatre or two, and packed dance-halls, having a whale of a time. At the weekend they just lounged around, doing very little but enjoying one another's company.

Ah, it was an easy time, a sweet time they had of it; those two weeks in London before the blitz and the fire bombs wrecked the place. It was never to be like that again. Not for them. No, never again.

And when it ended and they had to go the girls wept a little; which was enough to break

57

your heart.

'You will write?' they said.

'Yes, we will.'

'It's a promise.'

'Yes, a promise.'

But promises were like pie-crusts, made to be broken.

CHAPTER NINE

ORDEAL

About two years later they found themselves again in a lifeboat. It was not the Atlantic this time but the Barents Sea, which was perhaps an even worse place to be.

Their ship, the S.S. *Ryderson,* had been sunk by German aircraft when nearing Murmansk. There were twenty-three men in the boat, including the master of the vessel, Captain Andrews. Ten of these men died of frostbite and exposure before the boat eventually drifted ashore.

It was an icebound barren land they came to, and three more men collapsed and died on the foreshore. One thing only was there to give them any cheer, and this was a wooden hut some hundred yards or so from the shore. Inside it they found an iron stove, two bunks and a few cans of meat. It was obvious, therefore, that the hut had at some time not so long ago been in use, though it was cold and empty now.

They managed to light a fire, and they were able to keep it going with some packing-boxes that were lying around and driftwood from the beach. There were still some rations left in the boat, and they lived on these and the few cans of meat for more than a month, while three more men died, including the master. The remaining seven survivors included, besides Drake and Gray, two army gunners of the Maritime Royal Artillery, part of the Bofors gun team. They had shared a cabin with the DEMS naval ratings in the tween-decks of the vessel, with a sergeant in command. There had been a petty officer too, but neither he nor the sergeant had been seen after the ship went down. The surviving squaddies had been Liverpool dockers before joining the army, and they were as tough as old boots.

So when the food ran out and they began to starve there remained alive just the third mate, a man named Scott, two merchant seamen, two army gunners and Drake and Gray.

Even Gray, the eternal optimist, began to lose hope.

'So this is the way it ends, Eddie. Not with a bang but a whimper, as the saying is.'

'Eliot,' Drake said.

'What you mean, Eliot?'

'T.S. Eliot. He wrote it . "This is the way the

world ends not with a bang but a whimper."
It's in a poem called "The Hollow Men".

'Is that a fact? T.S. Eliot, huh? I never knew you read that stuff.'

'Well, now you do. And anyway, we're not done yet.'

'No, we're not. We could hang on for a few more days. But to what purpose? It all comes to the same thing in the end. *Finis.* Well, we've had some good times. Remember those two weeks in London with the girls?'

'We should have written to them,' Drake said. 'We promised.'

He had had two letters from Jillian. He had intended answering them but had never got round to it. And then no more had come from her.

A pity; but that was the way of things.

'Maybe we're being punished for it now,' Gray said. And he gave a laugh. But it was not a happy sound.

Earlier, before the food began to run out and they were stronger, they had made sorties from the hut, but had found nothing except a bare, treeless landscape, snowbound and scarred by ravines and totally devoid of any sign of human life.

Drake was having strange dreams whenever he managed to sleep; dreams in which he was forever stumbling into unknown surroundings from which he could find no way out.

He told Gray. 'It's rather like "Alice

Through the Looking-Glass". The more you try to get to a place, the further away it gets.'

Gray said: 'You're lucky. With me it's food. There's this bloody great table weighed down with roast beef and turkey and plum-pudding and God knows what, and as soon as I go to take a mouthful it just melts away.'

*   *   *

One day, when they had lost all hope, one of the army gunners, a little man named Preston, who had ventured outside the hut for what might have been a last reconnoitre, rushed back in, looking scared out of his wits.

'Bears!' he shouted. 'Polar bears!'

'What in hell are you talking about?' Gray said.

Preston repeated it. 'There's polar bears, I tell you. Big white things. They're coming this way.'

Gray went to the door and looked out. Then he gave a laugh. 'They're nearly here,' he said. 'But I never saw polar bears on skis.'

There were in fact four of them, in white clothing, and they turned out to be Russian soldiers from an army outpost some ten miles away. Because of the language difficulty this information was not obtained until later. But the evidence that those in the hut were survivors from a ship was plain for them to see in the beached lifeboat and the uniforms of the gunners.

It was Gray who put in words what all of them had to be thinking.

'We're not going to die. We've made it.'

CHAPTER TEN

SECOND TIME ROUND

They were in London again. It was survivor's leave for the second time round.

'We've earned it,' Gray said. 'We've earned it the hard way, and no mistake.'

Drake could not disagree with that. Because it had not been all plain sailing even after the ski patrol had found them. The hut, it appeared, had been used on occasion by trappers and seal hunters, but not for quite a while. It was fortunate that the boat had finished up on that particular stretch of beach; otherwise they would have stood no chance at all. Even so they were weak from hunger and there was a long journey ahead of them by sledge and sleigh before they reached the port of Murmansk.

They were to be in Murmansk for three months recovering from their ordeal. After that there was the voyage back to England in another arctic convoy which lost two ships in U-boat attacks. But now they were fit and well again. And they were alive. They had been very near to death. Other men had died, but they had lived; that was the main thing. They were alive.

'We are immortal,' Gray said. 'They can't kill us. I knew it all along.'

Drake remembered a time when he had not been so certain of that; a time when he almost lost hope. But he did not remind him of that. It seemed a long time ago now. And they had two weeks in which to enjoy themselves.

*   *   *

The trouble was that London had changed. Perhaps they had changed too. Certainly they were older, more experienced, harder, more cynical maybe. But chiefly it was London. There had been the blitz; much of it was in ruins. The Apex building had been gutted by fire-bombs and the business had gone elsewhere.

And the girls, Penny and Jillian; where were they? In uniform maybe; the flat in East Finchley occupied by someone else.

'We could go down there and see,' Gray suggested.

But they never did. They felt that it would be a wasted journey, a raking over of dead coals. Penny and Jillian were of the past, a different life.

London was full of spivs and whores and

deserters living on their wits. There were hordes of Americans too. It might be the friendly invasion, but they did not like it.

'It's not like last time,' Drake said. 'There's no magic in it now.'

It was a disappointment. Perhaps they had expected too much; something that had been lost and could never be recovered. Now and then the air-raid warning would sound and people would hurry to the shelters. If you travelled on the Tube late in the day you saw women and children and old men bedding down for the night on the platforms.

'Let's get out of here,' Gray said.

*   *   *

They went down into the country. They found an inn in a Norfolk village where they were able to get accommodation. It was not far from Norwich and there was a bus service that would take them into the city when they tired of the rustic life.

The landlord and his wife had a daughter who acted as barmaid. She was about twenty; a rather plump girl but not unattractive. She might also have been described as being of easy virtue. And she was impartial; she bestowed her favours on both Drake and Gray without discrimination. Sometimes she would accompany them on their trips to Norwich, and maybe they would all go to a cinema if there was a good film showing.

They were not sure whether her parents were aware of what was going on; but it was hardly credible that they could not be. So possibly they were broad-minded and happy to see their daughter enjoying herself. The mother was an excellent cook and rationing seemed hardly to have affected the lavishness of the meals she prepared for the two guests. They ate with the family and it was all very pleasant. One way and another they had no regrets for abandoning London for the remainder of their leave.

*　　*　　*

Molly shed no tears when the time came for them to depart; it would not have been in her nature. All she said was: 'Come again sometime.'

They said they would, but they all knew it was unlikely. And it might not have been so good a second time round. Better to settle for just the memory.

'And now,' Gray said, 'it's back to sea, I suppose. What kind of ship this time, I wonder.'

'Well, we'll soon know.'

'True. And we may not be so happy when we do.'

*　　*　　*

But as things turned out they were not destined to go to sea again for a while. And indeed the only ship they stepped aboard had not been on the ocean wave for a great many years. H.M.S. *Satellite* was a training ship which never stirred from its berth at South Shields, quite close to where the ferry from North Shields on the opposite side of the Tyne had its terminal.

Satellite had once been a sailing ship, but now the masts and rigging had gone, and much of the deck had been covered in by a kind of iron shed. From the roof of this structure rose stovepipes and other protrusions, while through ports in the ship's sides ancient guns thrust their impotent muzzles, aimed at nothing in particular.

This for two weeks was to be home to Drake and Gray while they took a course to qualify each of them for the gunlayer's badge of two crossed barrels to be worn on the sleeve.

There were ten men in their class: four naval ratings, two lance-sergeants of the Maritime Royal Artillery and four bombardiers. The soldiers were lucky; they were billeted in North Shields in reasonably comfortable private houses that had been commandeered for the duration of the war. Each morning they would come across on the ferry and travel back the same way late in the afternoon. The men in blue had to put up with the crowded and none too pleasant accommodation on board.

Their instructor was an old chief petty officer who had seen service in the 1914–18 war and seemed to have an affection for outdated weapons like the 12-pounder and the 4-inch breechloader. No one would have dared to suggest to him that the Bofors and the Oerlikon might be more effective at the present time.

The members of the class were instructed in the use of various other devices: small barrage balloons and kites to be flown from ships' mastheads, paravanes for dealing with floating mines, rocket projectors, and parachutes shot into the air with cables attached to catch the wings of low-flying aircaft.

Drake had little faith in any of these rather Heath Robinsonish contraptions, and Gray shared his opinion; but they dutifully went through the course. There was an examination at the end, both practical and verbal, and to no one's great surprise the army sergeants scored top marks. Both Drake and Gray passed creditably enough to be awarded their badges of proficiency as DEMS gunlayers, and each was subsequently promoted to the rank of leading seaman.

*   *   *

It was to be the end of their wartime

association. In their new ranks they were posted to separate ships and were to have no sight of each other for the remaining years of the conflict.

But they kept up the connection by means of an occasional letter, and it was in this way that Drake received the news that Gray had again been promoted and now held the rank of petty officer. He was now serving on board one of the big liners, the *Mauretania*. It was, he said, a cushy number.

'Ferrying Yanks across the herring pond,' was the way he described it. 'They're crammmed in like sardines, but we have decent cabins. Liverpool's our port on this side, and every three or four weeks we're in New York or Boston or Halifax.'

The liner sailed unescorted, but there was not much danger; even a U-boat on the surface would never catch a ship cruising at 23 knots and zigzagging all the way.

'There's three lots of gunners on board,' Gray wrote. 'Thirty of them are naval ratings, another thirty or so are army personnel, and about the same number of American gunners. There's an old 6-inch gun at the stern, a Bofors gun on each side of the boat-deck and Oerlikons here and there. Petty officers and army sergeants eat in a mess of our own and get waited on by a steward like paying passengers. Would you believe it?'

To Drake, still a leading seaman and still in

the convoys, it sounded like heaven. And there was more to it than Gray ever revealed in his letters, but which he recounted later.

It appeared that Gray and another petty officer, two Maritime Artillery sergeants and one of the American NCOs formed a syndicate to make money from the GIs taking passage in the ship. The *Mauretania* was at that time in effect a U.S. trooper, and therefore by regulation dry. However, the crew and the ship's gunners were exempt from this alcoholic ban, and it was the practice of the syndicate to buy as much whisky when ashore as they could carry on board. Then, when the ship was at sea, they would sell this to the thirsty troops at an exorbitant price.

'It's amazing,' Gray said, 'what a man will pay for liquor when he's forbidden to have it.'

'So you were profiteering?' Drake said.

'You bet we were. Hell! They'd got the money and had the need. We supplied the goods. Trouble was, now and then the Maurie would go to Halifax, and you know what that place was like.'

'Too bad. I grieve for you.'

'Of course we could always get cans of beer from the Pig and Whistle, the crew's canteen in the bows. The profit was smaller, of course, but not bad.'

The syndicate would also go through the ship in Liverpool after the troops had been disembarked, picking up anything worth having that had been left behind: army greatcoats, boots, gaiters, shirts, vests, pieces of equipment . . . Then they would take these items ashore and sell them to the spivs who hung around the docks. There were policemen at the entrance to the landing-stage, but they were no problem; they were only interested in contraband and stolen ship's stores.

Gray said he also made money playing poker with the Yanks.

'They were suckers.'

Drake wondered whether he did any cheating. Knowing Howard, it seemed more than possible.

He himself had had no cushy number, though the convoys were not being savaged so badly in the later stages of the war. And in the end both he and Gray survived. They had six years of it. It was enough.

CHAPTER ELEVEN

CALL OF THE SEA

They had gone in together and they came out together. They celebrated in London. It was winter and there were the scars of war all around: the rubble, the craters and the charred timber.

'It'll take a long time for the old place to get

back to normal,' Gray said. 'There'll be a lot of rebuilding to do.'

'Some people will get rich.'

'But not us.'

They were drinking beer in a bar not far from Piccadilly Circus. The bar was crowded and there were still a lot of uniforms to be seen. Demobilization had not yet been completed.

'So what do we do now?' Gray said. 'That is to say when we have to start working for a living again. Is it back to the old office desk routine?'

Their jobs were still waiting for them with Apex at the new head office if they wished to return. But was that what they really wanted?

'What do you think?' Drake asked.

Gray took a swig of beer, set the mug down and said: 'I think it would be just too damned boring.'

'Maybe. But what's the alternative?'

Gray answered with another question: 'Remember when we used to plan a journey round the world?'

Drake laughed. 'Oh, I remember. We were kids and it was just a dream. You're not suggesting we should do that now?'

'Not exactly. But we could still travel—and get paid for it too.'

'Now what are you talking about?'

'I'm talking about what we've been doing for the past six years, more or less. We're

71

seaman, aren't we? Well, the merchant navy is crying out for men. They've lost so many during the war, and ships need crews. They can't sail without them.'

Drake stared at him. 'Are you serious?'

'You bet I'm serious. Why not? The pay's not so bad, so I hear. A sight better than what we've been getting. Think about it.'

Drake thought about it. The idea certainly had its attraction. It would be a way of avoiding the looming office desk; which neither of them viewed with any enthusiasm.

'No need to decide straightaway,' Gray said. 'We've got time on our hands.'

'That's true,' Drake said.

But somehow he felt that already the die had been cast. The sea was calling them back, and they could not resist it.

*   *   *

The name of the ship was *Morning Star.* She was five thousand tons gross and flush-decked; a steamship that had been built in a yard on the Wear in 1936. She had been one of the lucky ones that had come through the war unscathed. At one time she had had a Bofors gun on a pedestal in the bows. The gun had gone now, but it was still possible to see where the pedestal had been sliced off by an oxy-acetylene flame; it had left a jagged steel scar. The 4-inch gun had gone too, and all the

72

other armament, as well as the life-rafts that had hung from the rigging in the days when they might have been needed at a moment's notice.

The ship was no longer a dull grey in colour, as she had been during the war. She had been repainted, and the funnel carried the coloured rings and lettering which identified the shipping company to which she belonged. She was now a tramp, going about her peacetime business without fear of torpedo, mine or bomb.

Drake and Gray went aboard in Bristol and signed on as able seaman, having taken a short course of training in their new duties. The crew's quarters, though far from luxurious, were reasonably good as such quarters went. Drake had experienced much worse, though Gray had known better on board the *Mauretania*.

The other seamen were the kind of mixed bunch they had rubbed shoulders with during the war. As former naval gunners Drake and Gray were regarded as rather odd fish, but there was no friction and they settled in quite amicably.

'There's one thing,' Gray said, 'we won't be keeping our eyes skinned for a sight of Jerry planes or tin fish. We'll be able to sleep easy.'

'I never knew you to sleep any other way Whenever you got the chance.'

'Well, you know what I mean.'

73

*   *   *

So the *Morning Star* set sail and went about her
business, and Drake and Gray went with her,
from port to port, taking on cargoes and
picking up cargoes, like a kind of postman of
the high seas. Wherever profitable trade
beckoned, there she went; and the two young
men saw parts of the world they had never
seen before; ports that had never figured in
the intinerary of the convoys or the big
troopships; faraway places teeming with dark-
faced people speaking in strange tongues.

'Any regrets?' Gray once asked.

'None,' Drake said.

And yet, was this strictly true? There were
times when he wondered whether they had
done the right thing. Admittedly it was an
interesting way of life; you never knew what
was over the horizon, what new experience.
But what future was there in it? They would
never be rich, that was certain. Nor could they
ever hope to become ships' officers; they had
come in by the wrong door for that. The best
they could hope for in the way of promotion
was to become in the fulness of time bosuns.
Truly it was not much to look forward to. And
would they stick at it long enough even for
that? He doubted it.

It was no surprise to Drake that Gray
should quickly have made himself popular in

the seamen's mess; it was the kind of thing that happened wherever he went; people of all sorts appeared to be unable to resist that undoubted charm. He himself was tolerated, but he knew he was no favourite. It did not bother him; he would never have tried to ingratiate himself with anyone; they had to take him as he was.

Of course Gray could spin the yarn. When he talked about that time when their ship was sunk in the Barents Sea and they were cast away on a barren icebound shore he had them hanging on his words. And how he did embroider the account! Half of it was lies, but only he, Drake, knew that. Then he would make them laugh with the account of his liquor racket on board the *Mauretania* and the way he had emptied the pockets of the Yankee suckers. They liked to hear about that.

'You're a regular Tom Bowling, aren't you?' Drake said.

'What do you mean by that?'

'He was the darling of the crew, wasn't he?'

He could see that Gray did not like it. He frowned slightly. Perhaps it had touched a nerve. But he said nothing.

They were with the *Morning Star* for nearly a year. They might have made it longer if something had not happened to cut short that particular part of their sea-going experience. And after that one thing was to lead inevitably to another.

75

CHAPTER TWELVE

DECOY

It happened in a small port called São Jorge in northern Brazil. The *Morning Star* was there for a short stay only, with no more than a small amount of cargo to discharge. On the last day before she was scheduled to sail all members of the crew were under orders to return to the ship by midnight. Experience had proved that this deadline was unlikely to be strictly observed, but as a rule seamen would trickle back aboard at various times through the night and early morning until the full complement was ready for duty when the vessel left port.

As a concession on this occasion the men were allowed to go ashore early in the afternoon, and Drake and Gray went with the rest.

There was not really a lot to do for amusement in São Jorge. It was no Rio de Janeiro. There were bars of course, and evening found Drake and Gray in one of these. They were sitting at a table and smoking foul Brazilian cigarettes, while listening with half an ear to the music being pumped out by a juke-box in one corner.

'What a hole this is,' Gray said. 'It stinks. The whole bloody town stinks. And this so-called beer is cat's piss.'

'Trouble with you,' Drake told him, 'is you've had too much of the cat's piss. In fact I'd say you're half pissed yourself.'

They had both drunk too much, he thought. And instead of making them feel happy, it had had the opposite effect. Perhaps it really was the town that was at fault; it was a dead-and-alive dump, to his way of thinking. Maybe it would have been a better plan to stay on board ship, read a book, listen to the radio. They could have saved their dollars.

*　　　*　　　*

That was when the woman came and sat down at their table without waiting for an invitation.

'You boys having a good time?'

She spoke English with an American accent. Seen from a distance in a haze of tobacco smoke she had looked younger. In close-up it became apparent that she was no chicken, though she had probably been a stunner at one time. She had jet-black hair and a swarthy complexion and brilliant eyes; and her mouth was a splash of raw colour that nature had never intended. She was not tall, but she had a good figure and moved with a certain grace.

'Do we look like we're having a good time?' Gray said.

She put her head on one side and gave him an amused look. Then she said: 'No, I guess you don't. So maybe I could help you liven things up.'

'Is that so?' Gray said.

'Yes, it is so. Are you interested?'

'Interested in what?' Drake asked.

'Look,' she said, 'why don't you buy me something to drink? What's that you've got there?'

'Cat's piss,' Gray said.

She laughed. It seemed to amuse her quite a lot. She had a gurgling kind of laugh, and the beads hung round her neck shook so that they made a little rattling sound.

'Well,' she said, 'we can do better than that.'

She signalled to a waiter, and he came over and she spoke to him in Portuguese. He nodded and went away and came back with three small glasses of some kind of liquor.

Drake paid.

'What's this?' Gray said.

'Never mind what it is,' the woman said. 'Just drink it and see what it does for you.'

She lifted her own glass and poured the contents down her throat in one swallow without batting an eyelid. Gray shrugged and did the same.

'Oh, boy! That's certainly got a kick. Like it was made from mule's blood.'

Drake took his more slowly, but it seemed to burn the lining off his throat just the same.

'Now,' the woman said, 'lets go some place else, shall we?'

'Where?' Gray asked. He sounded suspicious.

'Place where you boys will have some fun.'

'What sort of fun?'

'Girls.'

'You talking about a knocking-shop?' Gray said.

She looked puzzled. 'Knocking-shop?'

'He means a whorehouse,' Drake explained.

She gave the gurgling laugh again. 'Do I really look to you like a pimp?'

Gray looked embarrassed. 'So what are you talking about?'

'Come with me and you'll see. I promise you won't be disappointed. And incidentally, my name's Rita.'

'Well, hello, Rita. So what's in it for you?'

'My!' she said. 'Aren't you the suspicious one? Can't you take a helping hand when it's offered in good faith?' She turned to Drake. 'Is he always like this?'

'No,' Drake said. 'Quite the opposite in fact. You've caught him on a bad day. He's been sore all evening. I think it's the beer.'

'Oh,' she said, 'the cat's piss.'

And suddenly Gray smiled; just turned on the charm like a tap. 'Rita,' he said, 'I apologise. And since we're getting to be on first name terms, this is Eddie and I'm Howard.'

Drake could see that she was falling for the charm, the way they all did, especially the

79

women. Unless she was just putting on an act. And he could not be sure about that.

'So,' she said, 'how about it? Shall we go?'

'Sure,' Gray said. 'Sure, let's do that.'

*   *   *

It was late in the evening when they stepped outside, and the streetlamps were on. The air was warm and humid, and it seemed scarcely fresher than the fug inside. There was not a great deal of traffic at that hour, and the pavements were certainly not crowded.

'This way,' the woman said. 'It's not far.'

They began to walk, and before long they came to a narrow, ill-lit sidestreet. There was a car parked halfway along, and even in that dim light it looked as if it had seen a good deal of use since it came off the production line. It was undoubtedly of North American origin, with wings like shark fins and a lot of tarnished chromium plate.

Oddly enough, for no obvious reason at all, Drake had a sense of unease when he saw the car. It was the only vehicle in that narrow street, and it seemed too big for its surroundings. Two of its wheels were up on the pavement, and if they were going to get past it they would either have to step into the road or squeeze through the little space there was left between it and the wall on its left.

'Some people,' Gray said, 'will park just

anywhere. No consideration for pedestrians.'

'Never mind,' Rita said. And Drake thought she sounded a trifle nervous, though he could not think why. 'We can get past.'

She stepped off the pavement and skirted the car. Drake followed her example, but Gray squeezed past on the other side. They had taken a few paces beyond the car when Drake heard the doors slam. He turned and saw the two men coming at them, and he guessed in that moment that they must have been crouched down inside the car when the three of them went past. He knew then that he had been only too right to have that sense of unease at sight of the car.

But it was too late to think of that now; too late even to start running, to get to hell out of there. The men were on to them too quickly.

He heard Gray give a yell and guessed that he too had become aware of the danger all too late. The thought flashed through his mind that it was the woman who had set them up. She had been the decoy and they had been suckers to fall for the sweet talk. Hell, they had been around long enough to know the score.

Everything was in shadow, but he caught a glimpse of something in his assailant's right hand. It had to be a bludgeon of some kind. The man lifted it and instinctively Drake raised his arm to fend off the blow. In this he was only partially successful. The bludgeon struck him on the forearm, jarring the bone and glancing off on to the shoulder, so that he was hurt in two places.

He took a kick at the man's shin, and heard him give a grunt, indicating that it had inflicted some pain; but it did not stop him from having another go with the bludgeon, and this time he really scored. Drake took a crack on the side of the head, and this was the ace; it put him out like a blown candle flame, and for quite a while he lost touch with the world.

CHAPTER THIRTEEN

LONG WALK

He became aware that somebody had taken hold of his shoulder and was shaking it. It was his bad shoulder, and he was not at all happy at having it mauled, because it hurt like the devil.

'Stop that,' he mumbled. 'Stop it, damn you.'

'Oh,' said a voice, 'you've come to, have you. I was beginning to think you'd really snuffed it.'

The voice was Gray's, and when he opened his eyes he had visual confirmation of what his ears had told him. The thought came into his mind for a moment that he was on board ship and that he was being roused to go on watch.

But that notion was quickly put to flight when he saw above him the branches of trees and realised that the sun was shining through the leaves. He was aware too of a splitting headache and a tongue as dry as a strip of old leather.

Recollection of events not long past then began to come to him. The old car, the two men who had been hiding in it, the bludgeoning, the woman who had enticed them into the trap. Her above all.

'The bitch!'

'Ah!' Gray said. 'Memory returns, does it?'

'She set us up.'

'You bet she did. She dangled the bait and we gobbled it up. We went like lambs to the slaughter. Christ! You'd think we'd have known better. We're not kids.'

Drake's head was beating like a drum; it really throbbed and ached. He seemed to be suffering from the worst hangover he had ever experienced. His left shoulder ached too. And his forearm.

And then he became aware also that he was wearing nothing but a shirt and trousers and a pair of socks. No shoes. He glanced at his wrist to check what time it was and discovered that his watch was gone.

Gray said: 'They took mine too. They took our windcheaters and our wallets and all our loose change. They even took our shore passes, every damn thing.'

'Except our shirts and trousers. It's a wonder they didn't take them as well. Maybe we should consider ourselves lucky.'

'Lucky!' Gray said. 'Lucky! Jesus Christ!'

'What puzzles me,' Drake said, 'is how we were out so long. Looks like it's well on into the morning now. Would a knock on the head do that?'

'No need for it to.'

'Oh? Why not?'

'Roll your left sleeve up.'

Drake did so, baring his upper arm.

'See anything unusual?' Gray asked.

'Ah!' Drake said. 'I see what you mean.'

There was a puncture mark where the needle had gone in. Some bruising too.

'We were doped,' Gray said. 'They weren't taking any chances. Then they brought us out here and dumped us.'

'All that trouble for a couple of wrist-watches, a bit of second-hand clothing and a few dollars. Doesn't make sense.'

'Maybe it does to them. Maybe they thought we had more money on us. Maybe what they took seems quite a lot to them. Maybe they just do it for kicks. Who knows?'

'So where are we now?'

They were lying on coarse grass. A few yards away, where the trees ended, was a road of sorts, little better than a rough dirt track.

'God knows,' Gray said. 'Out of town; that's for sure.'

Suddenly Drake said: 'We should be on board. You know that, don't you? The ship's due to sail this morning.'

Gray answered sourly: 'That fact had not escaped me.'

'So we're in trouble.'

'Oh boy!' Gray said. 'You do catch on quickly, don't you? Let's go.'

They both stood up, and Drake felt twice as bad when he was on his feet. His head swam and his stomach seemed to be turning over and over like a butter churn.

'I don't feel so good.'

'And you think I do?' Gray said. 'You think I don't feel like death warmed up? But you can bet your life we're going to feel one hell of a lot worse before we hit town.'

*   *   *

They came to the road. It was worse than it had appeared at first sight; full of potholes which must have been hell for the springs of a car. Maybe few cars used it.

'Which way now,' Drake said.

'East. It has to be east to get to the coast.'

'Where's east?'

'Well,' Gray said. 'it must still be fairly early in the day. The sun comes up in the east, so look at the shadows and head away from them.'

'Supposing it's already afternoon?'

'Now you're being plain bloody awkward,' Gray said. 'Come on. Let's go.'

It was tough on the feet, but they soon had confirmation that it was morning, because as the sun rose higher the heat increased and they began to sweat.

The road did not run straight; it was as twisty as a snake. And it seemed to be very little used. They met one man with a mule, who gazed at them curiously but said nothing.

'This will never take us to São Jorge,' Drake said.

'Now tell me what alternative we have.' There was acid in Gray's tone—the concentrated kind. Maybe his feet were hurting him as well. It was not the kind of road to walk on with nothing but a pair of socks for protection against the stones.

*   *   *

They were relieved when they came to a metalled road; even more relieved to see a sign pointing the way to São Jorge. The only fly in the ointment was the distance given: twenty-two kilometres.

'It's going to be a long walk,' Gray said.

Drake agreed. 'And I have a feeling that my socks are already worn out.'

He suspected that the feet were blistered, but he decided not to make a check on this. They just had to press on regardless of the

86

pain.

There was a fair amount of traffic on the road, and they were hopeful of thumbing a lift into town, but their efforts in this respect were unfruitful. Possibly their appearance counted against them, and every driver seemed to be hell bent on reaching his destination in the least possible time.

'They must all fancy themselves as bloody grand prix drivers,' Gray said.

'Maybe it's the Brazilian temperament.'

*   *   *

They had practically given up hope when they struck lucky. An ancient Ford truck came to a halt beside them. It had not been travelling at the breakneck speed of most of the traffic; possibly it would not have been capable of doing so anyway. Sitting in the cab were a man and a woman, both rather fat and both middle-aged. It was the woman who poked her head out of the window and spoke to them. Since she was no doubt speaking in Portuguese they failed to understand what she was saying. They could only guess that she was asking them how they came to be there with no shoes on their feet.

Gray said: 'Inglese.' And he pointed at himself and Drake. Then he pointed in the direction in which they were heading and added: 'São Jorge.'

In any language that was easy to understand. The woman pointed at their feet and laughed. She was dark-skinned, with black hair as coarse as a horse's mane; and when she laughed her fat cheeks wobbled like jellies. The man laughed too, on a lower note. They seemed to find the situation far more amusing than either Drake or Gray did. Which was understandable.

However, when they had had their laugh the woman made a sign with her thumb which they took to indicate that they were to climb on to the back of the truck; and this they did without further urging.

There was not much room there for passengers. The truck was loaded with what appeared to be market garden produce. There were crates and sacks and a strong smell of onions; but the two young men were making no complaints; they were only too glad to be relieved of the necessity of walking. The back of a rackety old lorry was next door to heaven.

They came to São Jorge in the afternoon and thanked their benefactors, who still seemed to be greatly amused by their appearance; the woman particularly so. She jabbered away in her hoarse, throaty voice, and Drake had a feeling that she was half inclined to treat Gray to a hug and a kiss. Maybe it was only the presence of the man beside her that persuaded her not to do so.

Having left the truck, they made their way at once to the harbour. They had no difficulty in finding the quay where the *Morning Star* had been berthed, but the ship was no longer there; it had vanished from sight.

Gray began to swear, but Drake was silent. It was not a surprise to find the berth deserted, yet it was nevertheless a disappointment.

Always at the back of the mind had been the hope that the vessel's departure might have been delayed. Now it was certain that it had not. There was a sense of having been abandoned; destitute in a foreign land and without resources. It was not pleasant.

'So what do we do now?' Gray said. 'What in hell do we do now?'

Drake had no answer to that question. He sat down on a bollard and he could feel the throbbing in his feet and the sickness in his stomach. They had had nothing to eat or drink since the previous day, and his mouth was parched.

'We're in trouble,' he said. 'We're in bad trouble.'

'You don't have to tell me that,' Gray said. And he began to swear again.

Which was not going to help.

It was then that the boy turned up.

CHAPTER FOURTEEN

IN TROUBLE

The boy had even less on his feet than they had. He had no socks. It was difficult to tell whether his feet were dirty or not because they were black. The boy was black, without any of that shading into brown that many Brazilians showed. He was about four feet tall and as skinny as a tapeworm. He was wearing a pair of skimpy shorts and a singlet with holes in it.

He came up to Drake and Gray and stood looking at them in a speculative kind of way, as though sizing them up. He had a very steady gaze, and he seemed remarkably self-possessed for one so young in the presence of two perfect strangers.

'What you want, kid?' Gray said.

'Senhor Drake? Senhor Gray?' the boy said. He gave the names an odd kind of pronunciation, but it was near enough.

'*Sí*,' Gray said. 'That's us. Who are you?'

For answer the boy took a folded slip of paper from a pocket in his shorts and held it out to Gray, who took it and unfolded it.

Then, after he had perused it he handed it to Drake. 'Things are looking up.'

There was some writing on the paper, which Drake also read. The message was brief but to the point.

Your kit is at the harbour-master's office. Also arrears of pay. The boy has been paid but you can give him anything you wish. And damn the pair of you.

It was signed by the captain of the *Morning Star:* Josiah Hart (Master)

Drake felt a sense of relief. They were not destitute after all. They might be out of a job, but at least they were not down to a shirt, trousers, underpants and a pair of worn-out socks.
'Let's go,' he said.
They went.
The boy went with them.

*　　　*　　　*

The harbour-master's office was less impressive than its name. It was a small, single-storeyed, wooden building with a currugated iron roof, painted green. The harbour-master himself was slightly more impressive, if only because he had the largest black moustache Drake had ever seen. It was like an untrimmed hedge overhanging a pair of moist and bulbous lips.
He spoke a kind of English, which must have been useful in dealing with the captains

of British or American ships.

'Ah!' he said. 'So you are Senhor Gray and Senhor Drake, no?'

'Yes,' Drake said.

'Have you any proof of this?'

'What proof could we have? We've been robbed of everything. As you can see.'

The harbour-master shook his head sadly and pursed his lips. He seemed to find this most regrettable. Maybe he thought it reflected badly on the character of the port of São Jorge.

The boy chipped in then. Possibly he was recounting how he had been engaged by the captain of the *Morning Star* to look out for the two missing seamen and give them the note which was now in Drake's hand.

The harbour-master stopped him with a word. Drake was not sure what the word was, but it was effective. The boy lapsed into silence and made no more interruptions.

The man turned his attention once more to the seamen, and he appeared to have come to the conclusion that they were the genuine article. It was hardly likely that they would not have been.

'Your stuff is there.' He pointed at two large duffel bags which had been dumped in a corner of the office.

Drake had already noticed the bags and recognized them as his and Gray's.

'There is,' the harbour-master said, and it

seemed as though it gave him some mental pain to admit it, 'also some money.'

He unlocked a drawer in his desk, opened it and took out some paper money. Drake saw that it was in United States currency. He was gratified to note that there was somewhat more than he had expected.

The harbour-master licked a finger and counted the bills, dividing them into two equal portions.

'I shall, of course, need signatures.'

He had two forms already made out. He offered a pen. Gray signed first, then Drake. Then they took the money.

The boy was waiting expectantly. They gave him a dollar apiece; they were feeling affluent. The boy looked ecstatic.

There were gumboots with the kit. It was hardly suitable footwear for a port in the tropics, but for the moment they had no alternative. Drake felt the pain of blistered and swollen feet as he pulled the boots on, but his spirits were high. They were still in trouble, but not nearly such bad trouble as they had been in less than an hour earlier. They thanked the harbour master and left the office, shouldering the duffel bags.

The boy followed them for a while, but he soon tired of this and went off on his own. He had probably come to the conclusion that no more money was likely to come his way from those seamen's pockets.

Not far from the docks they found a seedy-looking outfitting shop; the sort of place that catered mostly for the lower class of customer. Here they each bought a pair of the kind of cheap elastic sided shoes that seemed to be popular with South American dockers. They bought gaberdine zipper jackets too, but they were economical with their money because they had no idea how long it would have to last.

After some searching they found a low-class lodging house where they were able to get a room at a rent that was suited to their slender resources.

'And now what?' Drake said. 'Do we go to the police and lodge a complaint?'

'You think that would get us anywhere?'

'You think it wouldn't?'

'Well, look at it this way,' Gray said. 'You find a police station. You walk in and try to explain to some disbelieving copper what happened to us last night; you speaking English and him not understanding one bloody word of it. Where does that get you? And even if he did pick up the gist of it, what then? Do you think he'd take any action? Not on your life, pal, not on your life. After all, what are the facts? That we were taken for a pair of mugs by a tart named Rita. That two thugs we couldn't see clearly in a dark side-street coshed us and carted us off in a car. That we came to some twenty miles out of town with nothing but our shirts and trousers and a pair of socks. The bastard would just laugh. He'd tell his pals about it to give them a laugh too. Couple of damn fool English sailors got taken for a ride. What a joke! You want that?'

'I guess not.'

'You guess right.'

'We could pay another visit to that bar. See if the woman is there.'

'And if she is? What then? Make a citizen's arrest? Take her to the cop shop? Forget it. Mark it up to experience.'

Drake could see that Gray was right. It was galling to have to take things lying down, but to do anything else was simply to invite more trouble.

'The way I see it,' Gray said, 'is to hope some ship comes into port short-handed. We might be able to work a passage back to England. You never know.'

To Drake it appeared to be a slim chance. But what else was there to hope for?'

*   *   *

A week later they were still hoping and the money was draining away at an alarming rate.

'We're in trouble,' Gray said. 'We're in bad trouble.'

Drake needed no reminding. To be on your beam-ends in London would have been bad enough; but in a foreign port where you did not even speak the language it was many times worse. They could have begged for help from the British consul if there had been one; but São Jorge was too unimportant a port to boast such a person. Here they were on their own.

'We shall have to sell some of our kit,' Gray said.

It would be a last resort. And at best it would only see them through a few more days.

CHAPTER FIFTEEN

ILL WIND

The S.S. *Cronus* came like a possible answer to a prayer. Drake and Gray were down by the harbour when she came limpimg into port with engine trouble.

Despite her classical name, the *Cronus* could hardly have been described as a ship of the upper class. Rust appeared to be the dominant feature, and it was no surprise to see that she was sailing under a flag of convenience—that of Liberia.

She was a vessel of about four thousand tons, and in her sooty smokestack it was possible to see where holes had been eaten into the metal near the top. There was dried mud on her anchor, and everything about her seemed to point to a long seagoing career in which she had gone steadily downhill.

Drake looked at her as the hawsers fore and aft were looped over bollards on the quay. And then he looked at Gray.

'What do you think?'

'I think,' Gray said, 'that this is one hell of a dirty little ship.'

'Nothing else?'

'Oh, sure. Plenty else. I think if there's the smallest chance of being taken on as deckhands we should jump at it, no matter what. Anything's better then starving.'

'I'm with you there.'

'So we give it a go?'

'We give it a go,' Drake said.

*　　　*　　　*

They did not try at once; there was no point in rushing things. And it was evident that the *Cronus* was going to be there for a while. But they did not wait long, since their need was great. It was the next day when they went on board the ship, and already the decks had begun to collect garbage, as the decks of ships tended to do when the vast dustbin of the sea was no longer available.

They found the mate overseeing some work on the foredeck. He was a thickset man, aged perhaps about forty. He had not shaved recently, and the stubble on cheeks and chin gave him ruffianly appearance. He was wearing shorts and a dirty white short-sleeved shirt, a greasy peaked cap on his head.

When the two Englishmen approached him he turned a jaundiced eye on them, and it was apparent that he had no great liking for what he saw. He said something in a language that neither of them could understand. It might well have been a demand to be told what in hell they were doing there.

Gray, without beating about the bush, said bluntly: 'We are seamen looking for work.'

He stared at them, and Drake wondered whether he had understood. He said nothing for a few moments; he seemed to be sizing them up and possibly not much liking what he saw.

Then he said: 'No. We got a crew. No vacancies. Better you try some other ship.'

'We have tried,' Gray said. 'We've had no luck. We need a job badly.'

'That's not my concern,' the man said. 'I got my own troubles. Maybe they worse than yours.'

'I doubt it, sir.'

'You can doubt it all you like. Makes no difference. Now I got work to do.'

He turned his back on them, and it was obviously a dismissal. Drake saw that there was no point in arguing. 'Let's go.'

Gray shrugged, and together they made their way to the gangplank. They descended it and found themselves again on the hard concrete of the quay. The faint hope that had flickered up like the flame of a candle for a brief while had been extinguished by the harsh words of the chief officer of the *Cronus* and they were back to the role of distressed British seamen from which there seemed to be no escape.

'She's a lousy ship anyway,' Gray said.

It was a case of sour grapes; but they both knew that a lousy ship was infinitely better in this situation than no ship at all.

'Maybe tomorrow there'll be something else.'

But hope was fading. They both knew that the chances of finding employment on board a vessel coming into São Jorge were so slim as to be almost non-existent.

*   *   *

Nevertheless, next morning they went down to the harbour again. The *Cronus* was still berthed in the same place, and there was no sign that she might be about to leave port. Indeed, there seemed to be very little activity on deck.

'I wonder where she came from and what kind of cargo she's carrying,' Gray said.

'Well,' Drake said, 'judging from the look of her, I'd doubt whether any of it is gold bullion.'

They were turning away when they heard a shout: 'Hi! You there!'

They halted and looked up; and there at the head of the gangplank was the mate of the S.S. *Cronus*. And he was beckoning to them.

'Come here.'

'Now what's he want?' Gray said.

'There's one way of finding out,' Drake said. 'Right then. Let's go and see.'

They walked to the gangplank and climbed to the deck of the ship where the man was waiting for them.

'You were here yesterday.'

Gray agreed that this was indeed so.

'Looking for work.'

Again there was agreement.

'Follow me,' the mate said.

They made no argument about that. It was as if suddenly a ray of hope had shone in the darkness of their situation. They would have followed him anywhere.

But they did not have far to go. Half a minute later they were in the captain's cabin and being presented to the master of the *Cronus*.

*　　　*　　　*

Captain Van Acker was a solidly built man with closely cropped fair hair, bleached to the colour of barley straw and a face so hard it looked as though it might have been made of brick.

The mate, whose name they discovered

later was Zokowski, and who came originally from Poland, said: 'The two seamen looking for work, Captain.'

Van Acker stared at them. He had the stub of a fat cigar between his lips, and he did not remove it when he spoke; he merely rolled it to one side with his tongue. As soon as he began to speak it was easy to tell that South Africa was his country of origin.

'You really seamen? You not just a pair of dockside bums looking for some easy money?'

It was Gray who answered: 'No, sir, we're not dockside bums, and I never knew a ship where deckhands could earn easy money. I'd sure like to find one.'

Van Acker laughed. 'What's your name, son?'

'Gray. Howard Gray.'

'British?'

'Yes, sir.'

Van Acker turned to Drake. 'And you?'

'Edgar Drake, sir.'

'Drake, huh? Any relation to Sir Francis?'

'Nephew, sir.'

Van Acker laughed again. 'You must be longer in the tooth than you look. Why you two on the beach?'

'We missed our ship.'

'It happens. What ship would that be?'

'The *Morning Star.*'

'I know her. Captain Hart. Right?'

'Yes, sir.'

'So how come you missed the boat?'

It was Gray who explained, somewhat shamefacedly.

'So,' Van Acker said, 'you got taken for a pair of suckers. What makes you think I want a couple of stupid bastards on board my ship?'

Gray answered coolly, keeping his temper. 'Stupid bastards maybe, Captain. But damn good seamen.'

'All I have is your word for that. You got any papers?'

'Nothing. Our wallets were stolen.'

'So I gotta take you on trust. Any kit?'

'Yes, we've got our kit ashore.'

'You better go fetch it then. And when you come back you can sign on.'

'I don't get it,' Gray said as they walked away from the ship. 'Yesterday we were told no hands were wanted. Today the Old Man tells us we're a couple of mugs, and then says we've got the jobs. What's going on?'

'Don't ask me,' Drake said. 'Whatever it is, we're in luck. We're not going to starve after all.'

Later they were to learn the answer to the question; and it was a simple one. It was the kind of thing that happened now and then. Two members of the crew of the *Cronus* had gone ashore the previous evening and had consumed more hard liquor than was good for them. On the way back to the ship an argument had started, and when they reached the harbour where the vessel was berthed words developed into blows and a struggle ensued.

It was a dangerous place for two drunken seamen to have a fight, and the result of it was that, coming too close to the edge of the quay, they lost their balance and fell together into the water in that narrow space between the ship's hull and the sheer side of the wharf.

A third man, who had been with them but had not been engaged in the brawl, raised the alarm; but by the time the two contestants had been pulled out of the water both were as dead as kippered herrings.

It was in this fashion that the need had arisen for two more hands to make up the complement of the vessel's crew.

For the present, however, neither Drake nor Gray had any knowledge of the reason why their fortunes had changed so suddenly. Not that this was worrying them. They were only too happy to accept what the gods had sent their way.

CHAPTER SIXTEEN

DEAD MEN'S BOOTS

The crew's quarters on board the *Cronus* were much as Drake had expected, judging by the look of the ship. They were down aft, under the poop. They were not good, but he had seen worse. There were six bunks in the cabin in which he and Gray were to be accommodated, and the dead men's gear had already been removed.

Of the four seamen who occupied the other bunks, one was a German, one a Greek and two were so cosmopolitan that it was difficult to discover what had been their country of origin. All spoke English with varying degrees of fluency; it seemed to be a kind of *lingua franca* throughout the ship.

These men received their new cabin mates with a certain degree of wariness, as was to be expected when two complete strangers came to share their quarters.

It was the German who addressed them first. 'So you the two new hands, huh?'

'That's right,' Gray said.

'What your names?'

Gray told him.

'I'm Schmidt,' the man said. 'Hans Schmidt. German. You English?'

'Yes.'

'Maybe you don't like Germans?'

'Why shouldn't I?' Gray said.

Schmidt gave a laugh. He was a stocky man, fair-haired, not bad-looking.

'We had a war. You forget?'

'No, I don't forget. But that's history now.'

'And you won, yes? Or was it the damn

Yankees? Or maybe the filthy Russians?'

Drake wondered whether Schmidt was trying to make trouble. It sounded like a taunt. Perhaps he still felt resentful regarding that defeat. Maybe he had been a Nazi. It might have been interesting to learn how he came to be a member of the crew of a ship sailing under a flag of convenience.

But Gray refused to be drawn into any argument and made no answer.

And then the Greek said: 'I am Nikos Costoulas.' He was a small thin-featured man with black hair, who looked almost too delicate for the life of a seaman. 'You been long in this place?'

'Too long,' Gray said.

'On the beach?' Schmidt asked.

'Yes, on the beach.'

'So lucky for you,' Costoulas said, 'what happen last night.'

'What was that?' Gray asked.

'You don't hear?' Costoulas sounded surprised. 'Hear what?'

'Two guys used to have those bunks you just take fall in the drink. Get themselves drowned.'

'Oh,' Gray said, 'so that's the way it happened. We did wonder. Yesterday there were no vacancies for a couple of out-of-work seamen. Today we're welcomed with open arms. Well, almost.'

'So you step into dead men's boots,'

Schmidt said. 'That is most bad luck.'

'You think so?'

'Oh, sure. Is well known fact.'

'Superstition,' Grant said. 'Old wives' tales. I'd say it was pretty good luck for us.'

'For now maybe. But later, you see.'

'I'm not worried.'

'So maybe you should be. You wait.'

'Oh, I'll wait,' Grant said. 'What else can I do?'

The other two men in the cabin were saying nothing; but they were listening. They were smoking hand-rolled cigarettes, and Drake thought he had never seen two more evil-looking characters. It came into his mind that they were the sort who would stick a knife into your ribs as soon as look at you. And of course all seaman carried knives in leather sheaths attached to their belts; so the weapon was always to hand.

He learned later that their names were Refalo and Zappa.

He learned too what cargo the *Cronus* was carrying. At the port of Talcahuano in Chile the ship had taken on board a mixed cargo that had included a consignment of small arms: pistols, rifles, light machine-guns, with ammunition. From Talcahuano they had sailed south to the Straits of Magellan, where they had picked up some bales of wool at the port of Punta Arenas. Thence they had headed northward, putting in at Montevideo and

Recife before being forced to put into São Jorge with engine trouble.

'And where do we go from here?' Gray asked.

'Havana.'

'Ah!' Gray said.

It was a non-committal expression, revealing neither disgust nor delight.

'You ever been to Cuba?' Schmidt asked.

'No, never.'

'Got anything against the place?'

'Me? Why should I?'

'Thought you didn't sound too happy about going there.'

'Right now,' Gray said, 'I'm happy to go anywhere, as long as I get fed.'

'Lotta rich Americans go to Havana,' Costoulas said. 'Just a few miles from Miami. You can get there in a motor-boat or a yacht in no time at all. They go for the gambling and the girls. There's this guy Batista who's in charge there. They say he's stinking rich.'

'And corrupt,' Schmidt said.

'Who isn't when they get to the top? Or before.'

'So why would Batista want arms from Chile?' Gray asked.

'Why does any dictator want arms?' Costoulas said. 'To keep him where he is. You bet.'

'They say there's a guy named Castro who's starting a rebellion out in the sticks,' Schmidt said. 'Maybe Batista's getting nervous.'

'Ernest Hemingway spends a lot of time in Havana,' Drake said. 'Goes fishing for marlin and tuna from a motor-boat.'

'Who in hell's Ernest Hemingway?' Schmidt said.

*   *   *

The bosun of the *Cronus* was a Swede named Bjornssen. He was about thirty, well over six feet tall and heavily built. He had fair hair and pale blue eyes and a thin slit of a mouth. Nicky the Greek, as he was known throughout the ship, said Bjornssen was a swine, but Drake found him civil enough at first meeting.

'You English, huh?' Bjornssen said.

'That's so.'

'And your pal?'

'He's English too.'

'Both able seamen?'

'Yes. We were in the Royal Navy during the war.'

He did not add that they had been gunners on board merchant ships. It might not have sounded so impressive. 'Good,' Bjornssen said. 'I need seamen who know their job. Some on board this ship, they just scum.'

Drake wondered whether that included the four with whom he and Gray were sharing a cabin. But he did not ask. It seemed rather strange to him that a man like Bjornssen, who

108

looked pretty smart and probably was good at his job, should be serving in a filthy old steamship like the *Cronus*. Surely he ought to have been able to do better for himself. But maybe there was some flaw in his character, some incident in his past perhaps, that held him back. One could never tell.

*   *   *

There was a carpenter too; an elderly, morose kind of man, who kept himself very much to himself. Drake never discovered his name or his nationality. The steward was a little stick of a man who seemed to carry the burdens of the world on his inadequate shoulders. He was never seen to smile and no one had ever heard him laugh. Perhaps being steward on board the *Cronus* was no laughing matter.

*   *   *

Drake had not expected the food to be of a very high standard; the cook looked as slovenly as they came. He was pleasantly surprised, therefore, when his first meal on board turned out to be far better than he could have hoped for. The fact that he and Gray had not eaten at all for some time would have ensured the acceptability of any food that was not absolutely disgusting; but it was not simply hunger that made the meal taste good.

'Nice to have a full stomach for a change,' Gray said. 'I'd almost forgotten what it felt like.'

*   *   *

With the engineers and firemen they had little contact. Now and then the sound of hammering could be heard coming from the engine-room, indicating that work was going on to put the machinery back into some kind of working order.

'I hope they know what they're doing down there,' Gray said.

'Why wouldn't they know? It's their job, isn't it?'

'Oh, it's their job all right, but on a ship like this old rust-bucket even the engineers may be no better than tenth rate. As well as the engine.'

'Now you're being cynical,' Drake said.

But he felt that Gray might well be right about the engine, if not the engineers.

*   *   *

Two days later the repairs were completed, the gangplank was drawn up, the hawsers were cast off, the propeller began to churn water and the S.S. *Cronus* headed for the open sea.

CHAPTER SEVENTEEN

CRAZY

When Drake took his first trick at the wheel it was in the second mate's watch. His name was Balboa. He was a small, rather plump man with a pudgy, slightly pockmarked face, delicate-looking hands and a soft voice. Anyone more unlike the bold conquistador of that name, who had been, according to legend, the first Spaniard to see the Pacific Ocean, it would have been hard to imagine.

'What is your name?' Balboa asked.

'Drake, sir.'

'You are English, I believe.'

'Yes, sir.'

'I have been to England,' Balboa said. 'London.' He seemed to be rather proud of the fact. 'It is a fine city, London. Wouldn't you say so?'

'Yes, sir.'

After that Balboa seemed to have exhausted his supply of small-talk and he lapsed into silence. He could have been Spanish, but to Drake it seemed more probable that he was a native of some part of the New World: South or Central America.

One thing was certain: the *Cronus* was manned by a remarkable mixture of

111

nationalities, and it might have been interesting to discover how they had all come together in one rusty old ship. Some of them were there perhaps because they were, as the bosun had said, scum. Perhaps it was not easy to get the best for a ship such as that. But good ship or bad, there could not have been one that was more welcome to him and Gray when they were at the nadir of their fortunes in the port of São Jorge.

*　　　*　　　*

The *Cronus* proceeded at a very moderate rate of knots in a roughly north-westward direction after she had lost sight of the Brazilian coast. If she had been sailing in convoy, as perhaps she had done in the past, it would have had to be one of the slowest. And even then she might have been liable to fall out because of engine trouble.

It was for this very reason that, five days after leaving São Jorge, the ship was no longer under way but was wallowing helplessly in a slight swell. There was little wind, and they were still near enough to the equator for the heat to be oppressive.

'This is nice,' Gray said. 'Now we stick here and sweat it out. And sweat is the operative word.'

'Well,' Drake said, 'you know what the old saying is. More days, more dollars. At least we're not starving.'

He had noticed something that struck him as rather odd in the past few days. Gray and the German, Hans Schmidt, seemed to have become quite matey. It was not what he would have expected; for at first there had been obvious friction between them. Yet now, on more than one occasion, he had seen the pair in what appeared to be thoroughly amicable conversation; though they always seemed to break up this conference of two when he approached.

He taxed Gray with this apparent turnaround in his attitude to Schmidt. 'I thought he hated your guts and that the feeling was mutual. Now you seem to be as thick as thieves. How come?'

'Oh well,' Gray said, 'it seemed damned stupid to be like that when we were sharing the same cabin and everything. And besides, he's not such a bad sort when you really get to know him. For a Hun, that is.'

Drake wondered whether Gray was being entirely frank in this matter. It seemed such a quick change of heart in both men. But such things happened, he supposed; and what other explanation could there be for those apparently friendly exchanges that took place between the two men?

Nevertheless, he still thought it odd, and for no apparent reason, slightly disturbing.

The breakdown did not last long. Appparently it was not so serious a matter as that which had forced Captain Van Acker to take the vessel into São Jorge. Within two hours the machinery started up and the *Cronus* was on her way again. Not many days later they were within a few hundred miles of the Windward Islands and apparently steaming towards their destination in Havana with nothing likely to disturb the tranquil continuation of the voyage, except perhaps a recurrence of that engine trouble which had plagued them before. But then something totally unexpected by all but a small handful of the ship's company occurred. And this was destined to change the fortunes of every man on board.

*   *   *

It happened just before midnight, when Drake was making his way to the bridge for his spell of duty. He had crossed the afterdeck and had climbed the ladder amidships when he heard a scream which was immediately cut off, as though whoever had made the sound had been suddenly gagged.

His immediate reaction, instead of continuing on his way along the starboard side, was to enter the accommodation by the doorway at the after end. Inside was an

114

alleyway with doors on each side giving access to the cabins. There was a light on in the alleyway, and he saw that one of the doors was ajar; the one opening into the mate's cabin.

He had just observed this, and his mind had registered the fact that it was odd, since Mr Zokowski would not be due to go on watch until four a.m., when someone came out through the doorway, and it certainly was not the chief officer.

It was in fact one of Drake's cabin-mates; one of the evil-looking ones; the one named Refalo. This surprised him very much, because the man should have been asleep in his bunk, since it was not his watch.

And then he remembered that he had noticed his absence when he himself had got up, but had thought nothing of it. Now, however, it occurred to him that Schmidt and Zappa and Nicky the Greek had not been in their bunks either. Only Gray had been apparently sound asleep.

Refalo came to a halt when he saw Drake and gave a grin. It was an evil grin, and everything about the man was evil. He looked crazy too. There was madness in his eyes, and in his right hand was a long-bladed knife, a seaman's sheath-knife. The blade of the knife was red from tip to handle, dripping with blood.

'Hah!' Refalo said. It was like a dog barking. He brandished the knife and Drake took a pace backward. The way Refalo was behaving, there was no telling what he might do. He seemed to be in a highly excited state, and with a bloody knife in his hand was obviously dangerous.

'What's going on?' Drake said.

Refalo grinned at him and made a gesture with the knife in the direction of the cabin from which he had just emerged. 'You go in there, you see.'

With that he gave another crazy laugh and ran off down the alleyway.

Drake hesitated. He had an aversion to entering that cabin, guessing what he might find; indeed, sure of it. But the hesitation was only momentary. Then he walked in and saw just what he had expected. The mate was in pyjamas. The jacket was open and his chest was bare, so it was easy to see the bloody stab wounds. There were so many it was obvious that the killer had attacked in a frenzy, driving the knife in again and again; maybe taking some vicious and perverted delight in the execution.

'God almighty!'

He had stopped at sight of the corpse, and he moved no closer. There was nothing he could do for Jan Zokowski; Refalo had made sure of that. You could not bring a dead man back to life.

But why had Refalo done it? Had he nursed a grudge against the mate? It was easy to imagine the seaman having a grudge against the whole world; but why Zokowski in particular? What was happening? Was something taking place of which he, Edgar Drake, was entirely ignorant? It seemed probable. But what was it?

He could hear the steady beat of the ship's engine like a throbbing pulse; and there were the usual creaking sounds that were always audible in a ship at sea; but there was nothing to indicate that anything out of the ordinary was occurring; nothing but the bloodstained corpse and the crazy behaviour of Able Seaman Refalo.

He had to make a move. He felt that he had been standing there for an age, though it could hardly have been more than a minute. He had been on his way to the bridge when the scream had diverted him, a scream which no one else appeared to have heard; no one except the killer himself.

So he had better go to the bridge now. There he could report what he had found and could give warning that Refalo had apparently gone murderously crazy.

CHAPTER EIGHTEEN

THE PLAN

There was another surprise in store for him when he reached the bridge. The wheelhouse was quite crowded. The third mate, Carlo Mendes, was there, though it was not his watch, and he was looking scared. He was a young man with a boyish appearance, and at this moment he seemed decidedly ill-at-ease, as though he had had a severe shock to the nervous system.

The bosun, Bjornssen, was there too, for no reason at all that Drake could discern; and Hans Schmidt also. At the wheel was Nicky the Greek.

The door of the chartroom was open, and Drake caught sight of the second mate, Balboa, in there, apparently studying a chart on the table.

It was Schmidt who greeted Drake. He said: 'You're late. What kept you?'

'What in hell's going on?' Drake said. 'Why are you here? And the bosun?'

Schmidt grinned at him. 'There's been a change of command. A takeover, see?'

Drake noticed that Schmidt had a revolver stuck in his belt, and he wondered where it had come from.

'Look,' he said, 'I've just come from the mate's cabin. He's been murdered.'

Schmidt showed no surprise at this revelation. 'Yes. That was necessary.'

'Necessary?'

'Yes. He might have caused trouble. Captain Van Acker had to be dealt with too. That was Zappa's job.'

Drake was stunned. He looked at Bjornssen. 'You knew about this?'

'Sure,' Bjornssen said. 'Is all part of plan.'

He grinned at Drake, showing his fine white teeth; and for the first time Drake realized that there was evil in this man too. It was a shock. Schmidt and Refalo and Zappa, nothing that they might do in the way of criminal activity would surprise him, but he had always thought that Bjornssen was a man you could trust. How wrong he had been!

Schmidt laid a hand on his arm and spoke confidentially. 'You're not needed here. Everything is under control. So why don't you go back the cabin and get yourself some sleep, huh?'

It was more of an order than a suggestion, and Drake saw no alternative but to obey. There was nothing useful he could do in the wheelhouse; for the present he had been made redundant. He doubted, however, whether in the circumstances he would get much more sleep that night.

He found only Gray in the cabin. To his surprise Gray was up and dressed. He was sitting at the table smoking a cigarette and with a mug of cocoa in front of him. It occurred to Drake then that he must have been awake and only feigning sleep when he himself had left the cabin.

'You're soon back,' Gray said. 'Don't they want you on the bridge? Well, I'm not surprised. You'd be rather in the way up there. In the circumstances.'

Drake stared at him accusingly. 'You knew, didn't you?'

'Knew what?' Gray asked, with an air of utter innocence.

'What was going on, of course. What else? It's what you and Schmidt have been talking about these last few days. It is, isn't it?'

'Well, yes,' Gray admitted, 'he did let me in on the plan.'

'But you didn't think fit to inform me. Why not?'

'For a very good reason in my opinion. What would you have felt it your duty to do if you'd heard about it? Wouldn't you have gone running to the Old Man and spilt the beans?'

'I daresay I might.'

'There you are then. That's what I was afraid of.'

'Why?'

'Because they'd have slit your throat, that's why. I saved your life, old boy. You should be grateful.'

'You didn't save the Old Man and the mate. I found Mr Zokowski just after our dear friend, Refalo, stuck the knife into him.'

'Ah!' Gray said.

'It wasn't a pretty sight. I hear that Zappa did the same sort of job on Captain Van Acker. And you knew this was going to happen, didn't you?'

'No, I didn't know. Schmidt assured me there would be no bloodshed.'

Drake did not believe it. Gray had always been a smooth liar when it suited him, and this no doubt was one of those times. But he did not pursue the matter; there would have been no point in doing so. The murders had been committed, and the victims could not be brought back to life.

'What I don't understand,' he said, 'is what it's all for. What's the object in taking over the ship?'

'Oh,' Gray said, 'there's a plan of course.'

'And you know what it is?'

'Naturally.'

'So tell me.'

Gray drew smoke into his lungs and his first words came out with little puffs of it accompanying them like punctuation marks.

'The plan, old boy, is to make us all rich.'

'Well, that sounds very nice, I must say. But

121

how is it to be accomplished?'

'For a start, the ship will not be going to Havana.'

'That goes without saying. Why else murder the captain and the mate and take over the ship? So where are we going?'

'Colombia.'

'Colombia! But that's the other side of the Caribbean Sea, isn't it?'

'Just so.'

'But why go there? Where's the point?'

Gray puffed out more smoke and watched it drift away. Then he said: 'Let me explain the plan; the beautiful plan cooked up by Schmidt and Bjornssen.'

'Ah, so the bosun was in this from the start?'

'Seems like it. Very deep character, that Swede. Who would have suspected him of being a subversive?'

'Who indeed?'

'But to get back to the plan. The idea is to anchor off the Colombian coast at some convenient point and send a small party ashore in the motor lifeboat to make contact with one of the drug barons, using either Balboa or Mendes as interpreter. A deal will be struck to exchange our cargo of arms for a nice big dollop of the cocaine or whatever; and after that's been taken on board we move over to the good old U.S. of A, which has a lovely big coastline on the Bay of Mexico. There we smuggle the stuff ashore and sell it for vast sums to one of the Yankee dealers.'

Drake stared at him in utter disbelief. 'You can't be serious.'

'Wrong, old boy. I'm dead serious.'

'But it's crazy. I never heard anything more crazy in all my life.'

'Of course it's crazy,' Gray said. 'But who's going to be hardy enough to tell Schmidt and Bjornssen that? Not to mention our other lovely cabin-mates. Safest thing for us to do is to go along with it and keep our heads down. I've vouched for you, so don't go and do anything stupid.'

'What could I do?'

'Nothing. That's the way it is.'

'Who else is in on this? Not the second and third mates surely?'

'No,' Gray said. 'They're just carrying out orders. Which they'll do because they're scared. They know what's happened to Van Acker and Zokowski, and they don't want it to happen to them. But of course they're necessary for the scheme to work because they're the only ones who can do the navigation.'

'How about the rest of the ship's company? Are any of them in on the plot?'

'No. But none of them will cause trouble; they haven't the guts. They'll soon know what happened to the top men, and our people are armed.'

Drake raised an eyebrow. 'Our people?'

In spite of himself Gray could not avoid an expression of slight embarrassment.

'Well, you know what I mean.'

'Yes,' Drake said, 'I know exactly what you mean.'

CHAPTER NINETEEN

CROOK

As Gray had predicted, no one on board the *Cronus* was hardy, or foolhardy, enough to oppose the mutineers. The wireless room was locked and Bjornssen kept the key in his pocket; so it was impossible to send out any message regarding the events that had taken place on board. The bodies of Captain Van Acker and Chief Officer Jan Zokowski were committed to the sea with little ceremony.

'My God!' Drake said to Gray. 'Do you realize what retribution these men could be bringing down on themselves if this business ever gets out?'

He could have added that Gray himself might be considered as one of the guilty party, since he had willingly gone along with the plot even if he had not taken a very active part in it. And it was certainly no very pleasant experience to be sharing a cabin with the two murderers, Refalo and Zappa. He could not

124

forget the knife dripping with blood in Refalo's hand and the mad look in his eyes. Suppose he or Zappa should take it into his crazy head to stick a knife into him and Gray while they slept. He could see no reason why either of them should do this; but did such nutcases need any reason?

He mentioned this possibility to Gray, who pooh-poohed the idea.

'You're becoming paranoid. They're not going to harm us. What would they stand to gain by it?'

'Pleasure maybe. Could be they get a kick out of killing. Like it's a kind of drug to them. You should have seen that bastard Refalo just after he'd stuck the knife into Mr Zokowski. He was really on a high.'

'Forget it,' Gray said. 'You worry too much.'

'Maybe there's plenty to worry about,' Drake said.

*   *   *

Under her new command the S.S. *Cronus* altered course to westward and steamed into the Caribbean Sea where buccaneers had flourished in the bad old days.

Balboa and Mendes were plotting the course under orders from Bjornssen and Schmidt, the twin leaders of the mutineers. The two officers were frightened men. They sweated a lot, and it was not simply from the tropical heat. Remembering the manner in which the captain and the mate had been done to death, they might well have figured that their own lives hung by no more than a thread. As long as they were useful no doubt they were safe, but suppose the time were to come when they had outlived that usefulness, what then? Dead men told no tales.

The engine-room staff were causing no trouble; they were keeping their heads down and going about their work as though everything were normal aboard ship. What else could they do when the new bosses went around with handguns that had no doubt been taken from the cargo? You did not argue with men who could hold a pistol to your head.

From the steward and cook no opposition could have been expected, and none came. Meals continued to be served regularly, and Drake was pleased to note that the quality had not deteriorated.

The carpenter spent most of the day hidden away in his shop, and he could be heard from time to time sawing wood or hammering nails. Drake wondered whether he was making coffins.

*　　　*　　　*

Despite the altered set-up Bjornssen did not forget that he was still bosun of the ship, and he saw to it that there was no slacking by the deck crew. He kept them at work and he was not slow to give Refalo and Zappa a lashing with his tongue. No doubt he still regarded them as scum, even though it was scum he had not hesitated to make use of when it suited his purpose.

'He should be careful,' Drake said. 'He could get a knife in his ribs.'

'Not him,' Gray said. 'He can look after himself. He's really one tough nut is our Swede.'

'Nobody's tough when there's a knife in his back.'

'So maybe he sleeps with his cabin door locked.'

'And maybe he needs to.'

'Oh, they won't do anything to him. They know he's the one who's going to see this thing through, so they want him to stay alive. He'd be no use to them dead.'

Drake thought this might be true. Self-interest was a powerful incentive. But he still believed the whole thing was crazy. 'It isn't going to work, you know. Things will surely go wrong. They're bound to.'

'Don't you believe it,' Gray said. 'It may seem a hare-brained scheme to you, but I've an idea it could just work out. I feel it in my bones.'

Drake had very little faith in the ability of Gray's bones to foretell the future, but he did not say so. Where was the point in arguing about it?

He said: 'Always supposing everything goes according to plan and you get wealth beyond the dreams of avarice, how is it going to be shared out? Does everyone on board get a whack?'

Gray shook his head. 'No. The way I read it, the engine-room boys don't come into it. Neither do the officers of course; and it seems the steward and the cook are ruled out. Basically it's the deck crew who are included. You and I will come in for a share.'

'I don't want any,' Drake said. 'It'll be dirty money, if it ever materializes. Which I doubt.'

'Ah, there's no such thing as dirty money. It's all the same, whatever way it comes to hand.'

'Anyway, I don't want it.'

'Well, if that's so, I'll take your share.'

'You're not squeamish, are you? I believe the fact is at heart you're nothing but a crook.'

Gray seemed not at all put out. 'What I believe in is looking after number one. That's the way of the world.'

Drake thought this was a cynical way of looking at things, but he guessed that Gray was probably giving a frank expression of his own philosophy of life.

And he had to accept it; because that was Howard Gray, and the man was his friend. With all his faults he was still his pal.

As to the efficacy of his bones as predictors of future events, however, it soon became evident that they were no more reliable than tea leaves or chicken's entrails, and far less so than the Weird Sisters who were such a bother to Macbeth.

*　　*　　*

They were getting near to the coast of Colombia, and there was an air of expectation in the ship. Everybody knew what had been planned and they were waiting to see how things turned out. And then, of course, the inevitable happened: the ship's ageing machinery broke down again.

It was a delightful scene; quite idyllic in character: the blue sky overhead, the pale blue water all round them, scarcely ruffled by any breeze, not another vessel in sight and this one moving gently up and down but not progressing towards its destination by so much as an inch.

'Oh, oh!' Gray said. 'Here we go again. Or rather here we don't go.'

CHAPTER TWENTY

A JUDGEMENT

Bjornssen was angry. He accused the chief engineer of sabotage. It was, he said, an attempt to frustrate his plans. The engineer, a dour, skinny, middle-aged man named Pedro Garcia, replied that there was no need to sabotage engines that were perfectly capable of breaking down of their own accord.

Bjornssen asked how long it would take to make the necessary repairs, and Garcia wrapped his shoulders round his ears and intimated that the matter was in the hands of God.

He was told to leave God out of it and give a straight answer to the question.

'How long will it take to do the job?'

'It may not be possible to do it at all,' Garcia said. 'Perhaps it would be advisable to radio for a salvage tug to come out and tow us into harbour.'

Bjornssen became incensed by this suggestion so much that he threatened to shoot Garcia and throw his body to the sharks. But the engineer was unmoved.

'You may do that if it pleases you, but it will not get the ship moving. Perhaps you should hoist a sail.'

He might have been purposely goading the bosun, but to what purpose? Maybe he took pleasure in it. Maybe he hated Bjornssen's guts; hated him for what he had done and did not care two pins if he goaded him beyond control.

But Bjornssen mastered his temper; though with an effort.

He said coldly: 'Do what you can. I depend on you to get things moving.'

Garcia shrugged again. 'A man cannot perform miracles. But I will do my best.'

*　　　*　　　*

His best did not get the ship moving that day. Occasional sounds of hammering came from the engine-room, but the ship's propeller remained motionless in the water.

Drake said to Gray: 'Fate has taken a hand in our affairs. This is one contingency that was not taken into account when the plot was hatched. As Mr Burns wrote: "The best-laid schemes o' mice and men gang aft agley." And this appears to be one of them.'

'That sounds to me very much like gloating,' Gray said. 'You're pleased this has happened, aren't you?'

'I must admit it doesn't exactly break my heart. I wouldn't want the bastards to get away with things.'

'All is not lost yet. The engineers may still manage to work the oracle.'

Drake was not sure whether to hope for that or not. As matters stood they were in a kind of limbo, and one could only guess what might happen next.

*　　　*　　　*

What did in fact happen might have been foreseen if anyone had been manning the wireless room and checking the weather reports that were coming in. They would then have heard a warning of the approaching storm that was destined to have such a great effect on each one of them. As it was they lived in blissful ignorance of this force of nature that was on its way towards them.

It came like a wolf in the night; stealthily at first. The sea felt it before anything else. The surface began to be troubled when no wind had yet come. Where it had been almost as smooth as glass, now it began to heave, moving in long, low corrugations which caused the ship to stir uneasily, as though from a vague premonition of the approaching ordeal.

*   *   *

Drake was in the wheelhouse, for watches were still being kept under Bjornssen's rule, even though the vessel was not under way. Mr Balboa, the second mate, was with him, despite the fact that in the circumstances there was little for him to do. It was possible, Drake thought, that he preferred to be up there with someone for company rather than brooding alone in his cabin.

He and Mendes were in an unhappy position. They must have realized that they were tolerated only because of their usefulness

132

to the mutineers; and they could have no certainty regarding what might happen to them at the end of the voyage. Drake himself had no idea of what Bjornssen planned to do if and when the drug transaction was successfully completed. Did he propose to sail away in the *Cronus* to some island paradise? Even if the machinery was put into working order by Pedro Garcia and his assistants there must soon arise the problem of fuel. A ship could not go forever without refuelling. But perhaps he intended to cut loose by himself and disappear with his newly gained wealth in the vastness of North America. One thing was certain: he would not give a damn regarding the fate of the others who had helped him with his coup.

Balboa seemed to become aware of the motion of the ship at the same time as Drake did. He remarked on it. 'Something is happening.'

Drake could detect a certain uneasiness in the man. And he felt it too. Until this time the ship had been almost rock-steady in the water, imparting a sense of security to those within her. Now it became apparent on what uncertain foundations that feeling had been based.

The movement of the ship increased steadily, though still no wind had fanned the rigging. But the second mate was not deceived.

'There is a storm coming. It could be bad; a

hurricane even. And without power the ship is helpless. There is nothing we can do.'

He was sweating. There was an oppressiveness in the air, which had become more humid. To the east the sky, which had been spangled with stars, had turned black, as though it were being steadily blotted out by an impenetrable curtain. This dark covering which was moving relentlessly across the sky was lit up momentarily from time to time by brilliant flashes of lightning, followed by the rumble of distant thunder.

And then the wind came. It came with such ferocity that it seemed like a ram hitting the wheelhouse. It shrieked through the rigging and the ship heeled over, as if cowering under the blow. Rain came then; at first a few exploratory drops which rapidly increased to a downpour like the overflow of some monstrous reservoir in the sky.

Drake and Balboa clutched at anything that would help them to stay on their feet, and the wheel, unmanned now, made sudden jerky movements, as if possessed with a spirit of its own.

Through the windows of the wheelhouse a picture of the foredeck of the ship was fleetingly but vividly revealed by the flashes of lightning. It appeared to be engulfed as waves broke over it, while the forecastle stood up like a steel island rearing itself above the surrounding flood.

Drake had to shout to be heard above the din. 'What can we do?'

Balboa shouted back: 'Nothing. We are helpless. It is a judgement.'

This seemed to Drake an odd thing to say He could only suppose that Balboa imagined that the storm had been called up by the Almighty in order to punish Bjornssen and his associates for their misdeeds. In which case the innocent would be suffering with the guilty; surely an inequitable way of meting out justice.

Suddenly Bjornssen appeared in the wheelhouse. He was wearing an oilskin coat, and water was running from it. He was bareheaded and his hair was drenched. For a moment he stood just inside the doorway, hanging on and simply staring at the other two. The light in there was poor; the electricity was supplied by a generator that was independent of the broken down engines, but it seemed as though that too was none too reliable.

'So,' Bjornssen said at last, 'we have a little trouble it seems.'

Drake thought this was pretty much of an understatement. In his estimation the trouble was far from little. But he said nothing, and Balboa said nothing either.

Bjornssen moved further into the wheelhouse. He looked out at the foredeck with the seas breaking over it and the foam flying here and there. He turned and looked at Balboa.

'What you think of this, huh?'

Again Balboa said nothing; just gazed back at him with hatred in his eyes.

'He thinks it is the hand of God punishing you for your recent misdeeds,' Drake said.

Bjornssen laughed harshly. 'Said that, did he?'

'Not in so many words. But it was the meaning. I think maybe I agree with him. In a way.'

'You too? Man, that's crazy. Did God put a spanner in the engines too?'

'Why not? If he can call up a storm like this, stopping a ship's means of propulsion ought to be child's play to him.'

'Ah, now you're kidding. You don't believe a word of it.'

'Makes no difference whether I do or not,' Drake said. 'One way or another we're well and truly in the shit.'

'You could be right at that,' Bjornssen admitted. 'It's certainly not a happy situation to be in right now. This is one hell of a storm and it's just playing with this old ship.' He spoke again to Balboa. 'What you think we ought to do, mister?'

'We could pray.'

This suggestion did not go down at all well with the bosun. He scowled. 'Now think of something practical. And keep God out of it.'

'We could send out a distress signal. on the radio. Ask for a salvage tug to come out from the nearest port.'

It was the suggestion that the chief engineer had made earlier, and it met with the same kind of reception.

'No.' Bjornssen was adamant. 'No radio signal. No salvage tug. We're on our own.'

'Then we are all dead men,' Balboa said.

*   *   *

The storm continued throughout the night with no abatement, and the *Cronus* staggered under the hammer blows of wind and sea. She was being driven westward, blundering along like a lame animal before the drover's stick. Drake hoped the hatch covers were battened down securely, for if one of them were to be swept away the hold beneath would be flooded and they would be in even more trouble.

Daylight came as a weak shadow of itself because of the heavy curtain of cloud from which the driven rain streamed down. All around were towering waves, from the tops of which spray was blown like horizontal showers of rain. Drake had earlier fought his way back to the cabin under the poop, but there was no possibility of sleep. Gray was there with Schmidt and Nicky the Greek. Nobody seemed to know where Refalo and Zappa were; and nobody cared. Drake would have been quite happy to learn that they had both been washed overboard.

'This is nice,' Gray said. 'This really is nice. Who wouldn't enjoy a lovely pleasure cruise in the Caribbean Sea?'

Nobody laughed. There was nothing funny about the situation in which they found themselves.

'Has it occurred to any of you,' Drake said, 'that if there hadn't been this stupid plan to get rich quick by a trade in drugs we might have been as safe as houses in Havana by now?'

Nobody answered him. It was not a subject any of them felt inclined to discuss.

CHAPTER TWENTY-ONE

DISASTER

There was no possibility of fetching breakfast from the galley. It would have been a wasted journey, since the galley was in a state of chaos and cooking was an impossibility. Drake and the others in the cabin made a meal of bread and cheese, which they had in stock, and they fetched water from the crew's washplace for drinking.

Hours passed and the ship continued to be driven westward by the storm, while performing the most unpredictable and erratic movements which made life on board a constant struggle to avoid serious injury. Even while lying on a bunk there was no comfort, and there had been little sleep for anyone since the storm had first struck the vessel with all its ferocity.

Drake wondered what was happening in the engine-room. It was scarcely likely that any work was being carried out on the broken-down machinery. So had the fires under the boilers been allowed to go out while firemen and engineers alike abandoned that possible death-trap and climbed the ladders to a higher deck? One could hardly blame them if they had.

The unwelcome thought came into his mind that the ship might founder. With all the stresses that were being put upon her, something must surely give way. Somewhere the water must find a way in and convert this thing that had the buoyancy to remain afloat into nothing but a dead weight of so many tons of steel and iron that must eventually sink to the bottom of the sea.

He mentioned this unpleasant possibility to Gray. 'Suppose the ship goes down?'

'Well suppose she does.' Gray said. 'What can we do about it?'

'Do you think it would be possible to launch the lifeboats?'

'Not a hope. Even if there was time, which would be doubtful, how could you do it in a sea like this? You can forget about the boats and just pray that the old girl stays afloat.'

Which was about what Drake had figured out for himself.

*   *   *

About halfway through the morning Gray lowered himself carefully from the upper bunk where he had been trying to keep himself from being too violently thrown around by the antics of the ship and prepared to leave the cabin.

'Where are you going?' Drake asked.

'To the bridge. I want to see what's going on.'

'You could have a job getting there. You know what the decks are like.'

'I know it's dodgy, but you made it the other way last night, didn't you?'

'True. But it wasn't easy.'

'OK, so it wasn't easy. Nothing is these days.'

'Well,' Drake said, 'if you're going I'll go with you. Though I doubt whether anybody's got a first-rate plan for getting us out of this mess. Balboa thinks we're all dead men. He wanted to radio for a salvage tug, but the bosun vetoed that.'

'I'm not surprised. He'll be a wanted man by the law after what he's done.'

'And you?'

'Not me,' Gray said. 'I took no hand in it.'

'Just a passive partner. Is that it?'

Gray frowned. 'You'd better not talk like that, old boy. You could be in the same boat.'

Drake said no more on the subject. At the present moment it seemed academic. There were problems far more pressing that needed to be solved.

He and Gray both donned life-jackets before leaving the cabin. It seemed a reasonable precaution to take in the circumstances, though it might take a great deal more than a padded jacket to preserve their lives in the present situation.

When they stepped outside the first thing they noticed was that it was no longer raining.

'Hey-ho!' Gray said. 'Looks like it's clearing up. Maybe the worst is over.'

To Drake that seemed to be somewhat over-optimistic. Though the wind too seemed to have decreased slightly in strength and away to the east there was a break in the clouds, the sea appeared to be in as great a turmoil as ever. Nevertheless, the storm was evidently passing, and the ship was still afloat. That was the main consideration.

'Come on,' Gray said. 'Forward march.'

The afterdeck was tilted to port and seas were gushing over the bulwark, so they decided to make a run for it on the starboard side. They were halfway across when the ship made another erratic shift which caught Drake off-balance and threw him forward on to hands and knees. A rush of water rolled him into the scuppers, and he felt a blow on the shoulder which numbed his right arm. He struggled to get up, but was not making much of a success of it when Gray stepped in to lend a much needed hand.

Gray took a grip on his life-jacket and hauled him to his feet, shouting in his ear.

'Let's go, let's go.'

They made it to the ladder leading to the higher deck and grabbed the handrails and hung on. Gray went up first and Drake followed, drenched from head to foot.

'You all right?' Gray asked.

'More or less.'

'That was a nasty tumble. Better be more careful next time. You could break a leg.'

'I'll bear it in mind,' Drake said. He guessed he was going to have a stiff shoulder for a time, but things could have been worse. 'Where now?'

'Up to the bridge, I think,' Gray said. 'Come on.'

They were moving in that direction when something happened that altered the entire situation in a moment. The ship gave a lurch to port and then came to a shuddering stop, as though she had encountered some immovable obstruction. There was a tremendous screeching, grinding noise, and she had heeled over on to her port side and was lying there, apparently powerless to right herself.

Drake and Gray had been staggered by the

impact but managed to grab handholds and stay on their feet. They waited for the deck, which was now sloping fairly acutely, to tilt back the other way as it had been doing before, but this time there was no such counter movement.

'We hit something,' Gray said; and there was a note of awe in his voice, as if he were thinking of what it could be that was capable of bringing to a halt a drifting four thousand ton ship and hold it there. 'We bloody well hit something.'

But what?

And then the answer came immediately on the heels of the question.

A reef.

It had to be that or a rock. And a coral reef in those waters seemed the more likely.

'Now we are in trouble,' Gray said. 'Real trouble.'

There could be no doubt about that. The ship was still making spasmodic movements as successive waves struck her on the starboard side, and there were ominous grating noises to accompany the slight shifting in her position.

From the place where Drake was standing he could see that the deck was sloping away from him in the direction of the port rails. These at present were above water, and beyond them he caught a glimpse now and then of something solid breaking the surface as the sea washed around it in a flurry of creamy foam. This was undoubtedly the upper part of the reef on which the *Cronus* had come to grief. Driven by wave and wind she had stumbled broadside on against this natural wall and now lay with her port side in contact with the underwater obstruction, the steel plates of her hull grinding against it with a noise that was ominous in the extreme.

'Do you think we've been holed?' Drake said.

It seemed a dreadful possibility that somewhere, perhaps in the midships section, the hull had been stove in and that even now seawater was flooding the engine-room.

'We'll be lucky if we haven't,' Gray said. 'That was an almighty crunch. If you ask me, the old girl's had it. She's never going to get out of this one. It's curtains for *Cronus* in my opinion. Maybe curtains for us too.'

'So what do we do now?'

'May as well go where we were going. Hear what our masters have to say about the situation. Not that I put much faith in any of that lot.'

They climbed to the boat-deck and clawed their way to the bridge ladder. Drenching spray was still being flung to that height, and every now and then a shudder, as of fear, seemed to pass through the vessel. Drake had the impression that she was settling ever more deeply in the water.

They found nobody on the starboard wing

of the bridge, but the door to the wheelhouse was standing open and they could see that a number of people were inside. They went in and found the two surviving deck officers, Balboa and Mendes, along with Bjornssen and Schmidt and the carpenter, who had obviously been enticed out of his usual retreat by the turn of events. Everyone was clinging to something to maintain a balance on the sloping deck, a handrail, a door handle, even the wheel and the binnacle.

Nobody took much notice of the new arrivals; they were all far too engrossed in a discussion that had already been going on. The chief engineer was there, and Drake gathered that he had reported that water was pouring into the engine-room through a massive hole in the ship's hull. It was his contention that nothing could now save the ship and that there was not a great deal of time left before she slid off the reef and sank in deep water.

Balboa, who, as senior surviving officer, should have been in command, was inclined to agree with this contention; but Bjornssen, who had by force of arms taken over effective control, still stubbornly refused to accept the view that all was lost. For him there was so much at stake. He was a man obsessed with one overriding passion: the desire for money. He would not believe that by reason of circumstances beyond his control that desire could never now be satisfied.

'The ship is still afloat, The storm is dying down, Tomorrow—'

'Tomorrow,' Garcia said, 'none of us will be here.'

Bjornssen turned on him in a fury. 'It was your damned engines.' He choked, as if the words of condemnation stuck in his throat.

He blamed the engineer and not himself for the situation in which they found themselves. He was blind to his own culpability. He had had two men murdered to further his aims, but it was evident that this was not on his conscience.

'Perhaps,' Balboa suggested diffidently. 'we should think of launching the boats.'

Bjornssen looked at him with contempt. 'In this sea?'

'It may be necessary. If the ship goes—'

'The ship will not go.'

It was as though Bjornssen believed that by his will alone he could keep the vessel afloat.

Gray spoke to Drake: 'He's mad. Stark staring. Let's go and see what it looks like on the other side.'

CHAPTER TWENTY-TWO

RABBLE

Supporting themselves by the scrubbed teak rail on the forward side, they made their way down the sloping wing of the bridge. With the vessel listing so heavily to port, the end of the wing projected over the reef and they could see below them the churned-up water capped with white foam. From time to time peaks of coral could be glimpsed above the surface, only to be almost immediately engulfed again.

Ironically, now that the damage had been done, the storm did appear to be moving away. The sun had come out and was pouring down warmth upon the ship that so recently had received only the lashing of rain from overhead. Steam rose from those parts of the vessel that were above water, and Drake felt hot under his life-jacket in spite of the drenching he had taken.

He wondered whether there had been any attempt in the engine-room to plug the hole through which the water was entering. Perhaps it was far too big for that. Certainly the chief engineer had given no hint that there was any possibility of carrying out an operation of this kind. He seemed resigned to the inevitable.

'Suppose,' Drake said, 'the engine-room

gets completely flooded. Would that be enough in itself to sink the ship?'

'I've no idea,' Gray said. 'But there are other factors to be taken into account. There could be water getting into one or two of the holds as well for all we know.'

'Looking on the bright side.'

'Frankly,' Gray said, 'I think it would be difficult to find a bright side in this situation.'

Drake thought he was about right at that. Unfortunately.

He looked aft and could see that some of the crew were gathered on the poop. As far as he could tell, they were not doing anything. What was there that they could usefully do? Perhaps they were resigned to their fate.

But a moment later he guessed that they must have come to some decision, because they were descending the ladder on the starboard side and making their way along the deck towards the bridge.

'I guess they want to know what's going on up here,' Gray said. 'I doubt whether their welfare is much on the bosun's mind at this moment in time.'

'Or on Balboa's either, if it comes to that.'

*   *   *

Suddenly the ship gave another of those jerky movements that made such a harsh, rasping sound and did nothing to calm the nerves. This

148

time it seemed to go on longer than usual, and Drake wondered whether it was going to be the final disastrous move that would plunge the ship and all those within her to their watery grave. He gripped the rail and held his breath, and the movement stopped. The ship was lower in the water, but there was still a large part of her above the surface.

It was, however, the last straw as far as Balboa was concerned. Screwing up his courage to the limit, he defied Bjornssen and gave the order to abandon ship.

In this he had the backing of all except the bosun; and though Bjornssen might rage, there was nothing he could do about it. Except perhaps to shoot the second mate. He might well have been willing to do just this; but it would have been ineffective in preventing the others from taking to the boats and leaving. So he raved, but finally went with the crowd. Perhaps he was perceptive enough to realize that it was the only hope he could have of saving his life.

*   *   *

The motor lifeboat was the one on the port side of the boat-deck, and it was this that they went to first. It was a rabble; there was no order to it. Balboa should have been in charge, but he had no authority over a set of men who were undoubtedly starting to panic. They should have been drilled in the correct procedure; but there had been no lifeboat drill since Drake and Gray had come on board. So now everyone rushed to the port side of the steeply sloping boat-deck.

Drake and Gray stood aside and watched with contempt as the heavy boat was hauled up from the chocks and swung outboard on the davits. They could hear Bjornssen's voice as he yelled at the men in an attempt to put some order into the operation. It appeared that he was now going along wholeheartedly with the decision to abandon ship, since opposition to it had proved useless. But even his shouting and cursing could do little to make the launching of the boat anything but a botched job.

The angle of the deck was so acute that, with the davits leaning out from the ship's side, there was a wide gap between the suspended boat and the rails. Some of those not manning the falls tried to jump into the boat as it went down. A few of them were successful, but others missed the mark and fell into the sea.

The boat itself was not going down with a level keel, and so steep was the tilt that some of the men in it were tumbled into a heap in the bows. The lower end hit the water first and the other followed. Somehow the hooks on the pulley blocks at each end were released, but this was premature, since a number of those who wished to get into the boat were left on deck.

In the event it was perhaps fortunate for them, since the boat itself was becoming unmanageable in the surging water. Someone seemed to be trying to start the motor, but without success, and a moment later a wave lifted the boat and carried it away from the ship's side. It travelled about twenty yards, and then it appeared to strike some underwater obstruction which brought it to a halt. Some of those in it were still trying to work it free with the help of oars when another wave engulfed it.

Drake was gratified to recognize among those who were now struggling for their lives in the flood were Refalo and Zappa.

He felt Gray's hand on his arm.

'This is a shambles,' Gray said. 'Come with me.'

Drake made no argument. He was sickened by what he had seen; the panic and the incompetence; and he followed Gray willingly.

They clambered up the inclined deck to the starboard side, and then made their way aft to the poop. Gray led the way into the cabin, deserted now. There the first thing he did was to take off his lifejacket.

'These damned things are not going to save our lives. They just get in the way.'

He now began to pack his kit into a duffel bag; and Drake, still asking no questions, followed suit. He was sure that Gray had some plan in mind which would be revealed in due course.

*   *   *

It was while they were thus engaged that the ship moved again, with more of that rasping sound which was so terrifying to hear. For a moment they both froze, waiting for the movement to cease and fearing that this might perhaps be the end of the *Cronus.*

Drake gave a sigh of relief when in fact the movement did come to a stop and the only sound was that of the sea belabouring the stricken vessel.

'She won't last much longer,' Gray said. 'I thought she might be going that time. We'd better hurry.'

In addition to the kit they took some provisions: bread and cheese, biscuits, stowed in a canvas bag; drinking water in screw-top bottles.

'Now let's go.'

Carrying their loads they left the cabin and climbed to the deck above. By this time Drake had already guessed what Gray had in mind. Standing on end and lashed to the back of the deckhouse was a raft. It was the kind that all merchant ships had carried during the war, usually attached to the rigging, as an addition to the lifeboats. Most had been removed now, but somehow this one had survived.

'You think this will be better than a boat?'

'Don't you?' Gray said. 'You saw what happened back there. I wouldn't trust myself with that lot.'

Together they released the raft from the lashing that held it and let it fall to the deck. It was a large rectangular object, comprising a slatted wooden frame which enclosed a number of airtight metal drums that added to its buoyancy. In the centre was a narrow gully or trough between the drums. There were compartments in each end of the trough, which in wartime had held provisions and first-aid kit and distress flares; but all these had long gone. Drake and Gray dumped their gear in the trough, and again felt the ship move, again with that ominous rasping sound. And again she came to rest.

'Maybe next time,' Gray said. 'There must be a lot of water getting into her, and my feeling is that she's just sliding off the reef.'

With some difficulty they shifted the heavy raft closer to the stern and clear of any obstruction. They could hear some shouting coming from the direction of the bridge, and when they moved across and leaned over the starboard rails they could see that an attempt was being made to launch the second lifeboat. Here the problem was that the heavy listing of the ship made it impossible to swing the boat clear of the hull even at the full extent of the davits. Those in the boat were using the oars as levers; but as soon as they gained a bit of leeway another wave would come along and smash the boat back against the side.

They were still working on it with little success when the ship began to move again.

'This is it,' Gray said. 'This is the big one. Time for us to leave.'

CHAPTER TWENTY-THREE

CRY IN THE NIGHT

They got onto the raft and sat with their feet in the trough. And Drake knew that Gray had been right: this time the ship was really going, and for her it would be the final voyage.

He had a strange sense of the inevitability of it all; a feeling that this had to happen; as if every incident since they joined the *Cronus* had been leading to this conclusion. He listened to the usual rasping sound and the slap of the waves; and he took a grip on the slats and waited for the water to come dribbling over the poop.

Oddly, the deck appeared to be sloping less acutely as the ship sank lower. And then the water was all around them and the raft was afloat. For a moment it seemed that a corner of it might catch under the taffrail, but together they managed to push it off and it floated free.

Drake wondered whether as the ship sank it would suck the raft down with it; but in the event this did not happen. And in fact, just after the two had parted company, the ship stopped sinking and came to rest with her mastheads visible above the surface from time to time as the waves rolled over her. It seemed likely therefore that she had come to rest on some underwater shelf that was part of the reef. And there she might remain until gradually broken up by the action of the waves.

Not that it made any difference to the situation. A ship with only its mastheads above water was of no more use to the survivors than one totally submerged.

Drake looked for the second lifeboat and saw that it was afloat but that it was keel uppermost. There were two or three men clinging to it, and the heads of others could be seen here and there in the water. Cries for help could be faintly heard though those who cried out might as well have saved their breath, for no help was likely to come to them.

'They're done for,' Gray said.

He spoke without emotion, as though merely stating a fact that in no way affected him.

Drake could not disagree with him. The two lifeboats might have been useful if they had been launched successfully; but with no one capable of taking command and seeing that things were done in an orderly fashion there had been no chance of that. And the fact was that though he and Gray were for the moment alive and not threatened with imminent death, the future for them also looked far from rosy.

The raft rose and fell with the motion of the waves, but it was making no rapid movement away from the wreck, and they were helpless to propel it one way or another.

Suddenly Gray said: 'Look there.'

Drake turned his gaze in the direction indicated and saw what had caught his attention. Three men were swimming, and undoubtedly they were heading for the raft. It was no easy feat to swim at all in such waters, but they were making headway and the distance was not great.

'Hell and damnation!' Gray said. 'Looks like we could have a boarding party. And that's something we do not want. Two's company, but five would be too much of a bloody crowd.'

'Well, what can we do about it if they get here?'

'We can give them a kick in the teeth, that's what. Who thought of this raft? Who got it afloat? We did. Certainly not them. So we're entitled to keep it to ourselves. That's my opinion.'

'But we can't just let them drown.'

'Why in hell not? There's others doing just that. What's so special about these three?'

Drake said nothing more. He was not sure just how Gray would act if the three men did reach the raft. Would he really kick them in the teeth? Maybe he would.

And then he saw that the three men had been reduced to two. One of them had failed to make it in that still rather turbulent sea. But still the others came on.

There was a small axe attached to the raft with a cord. It was of the type used by firemen, with a blade on one side and a spike on the other. Gray cut the cord with his sheath-knife and took the axe in his hand.

'You can't do it,' Drake said.

'Who says I can't?'

'They're human beings.'

'So they have to die sometime. We all do. It's the one thing we know for certain.'

The two swimmers were close to the raft now; but Drake was unable to see who they were. He and Gray were kneeling down to keep their balance on that unstable platform, and both were watching the laboured approach of the swimmers. A little later one of them had come close enough to get a grip on one of the slats of the raft. The other was close behind him and soon found a handhold also.

'Well,' the first man said; and he was breathing heavily after his exertions, 'I certainly am glad to get here. So you took the damn raft. You two clever boys, I'll say that.' It was the bosun, Sven Bjornssen.

The other man said: 'Good thing we swim. Dead men else.' The other man was Hans

157

Schmidt.

Drake reflected that of all the men who had been on board the *Cronus* these were the two he would least have wished to see. With the possible exception of Refalo and Zappa.

Bjornssen spotted the hatchet in Gray's hand. 'What you do with that?'

'Maybe I use it to repel boarders,' Gray said. 'Maybe there's no room for more than two on this raft. I didn't see you lending a hand to get it afloat. So what claim have you to a share of the limited accommodation?'

Schmidt said: 'We're shipmates. You can't leave us to drown.'

'Who says I can't? There's plenty others drowned. So what's so special about you two?'

Bjornssen appealed to Drake. 'You got a heart. You know you have to help us. Law of the sea.'

Drake thought this was a bit rich, coming from a man who had been so contemptuous of the laws of the sea or the land when he had seized control of the *Cronus* and had the captain and mate murdered. But he still found it impossible to bring himself to send these two men to their death, villains though they were. So he stretched out a hand and helped the bosun climb on board the raft.

Gray looked on in disgust but made no attempt to use the hatchet. He just said:

'You'll regret this, Eddie. You're bringing trouble on board, as sure as God made little

158

apples.'

'You're wrong,' Bjornssen said. 'You get no trouble from us. Help maybe, but no trouble. I promise.'

Meanwhile Schmidt had managed to get himself on board without assistance. The raft had tilted while he was doing so, but then it righted itself as the four men arranged their positions on the slats. So, with its human cargo the raft rose and fell as the waves moved it; and slowly it moved away from the wreck and the scene of that final disaster which stemmed almost entirely from the greed and inhumanity of two of these four survivors.

*   *   *

The sun was hot now; the wind was a zephyr; and gradually the sea calmed. Wet clothes steamed in the sunshine and dried out. The men on the raft eyed one another warily. There was not much trust on that small floating island, and none of them could have expected that there would be.

Bjornssen looked at the bag. 'What you got in there?'

'What do you think?' Gray said.

'Food maybe. You take precautions. Don't mean to starve. Water in the bottles too, I see.'

'You do a lot of observing. If there is food and water it wasn't put here for you and him.' Gray jerked a thumb at Schmidt. 'You better

159

remember that.'

'So you feed while we starve? Right?'

'Dead right,' Gray said.

But Drake knew it would not be like that. He knew that now that the other men were on the raft the meagre provisions would have to be shared with them. Which meant that they would be consumed twice as quickly.

And there would be conflict; no doubt about that. It was not going to be one happy little party adrift on those few square feet of timber and metal.

*   *   *

The day passed slowly. They did not talk much. They sat and watched the horizon; and in all that wide expanse of sea they could discern no indication that they were not alone on its surface.

Later in the day Gray dealt out a small amount of bread and cheese to each of them and a few inches of water in an enamel mug. He did so grudgingly, knowing that there would be trouble if he tried to exclude the late comers. In the evening he repeated the exercise; and Schmidt complained about the meagreness of the ration.

Gray told him to shut his trap. 'You're lucky to be getting anything. You're damned lucky to be alive. We saved your life, and to my way of thinking it was never worth the saving.'

160

Rather to Drake's surprise, Bjornssen backed Gray in this. 'You nothing but a goddam Nazi on the take. Maybe we should shove you overboard and have done with it. More for us then.'

Schmidt retaliated by calling Bjornssen a filthy Swedish bastard; and they went at it hammer-and-tongs for awhile. It was evident that the two ringleaders of the mutiny of the *Cronus* had no love for each other now that the enterprise had failed. It seemed for a while that words might lead to blows, but it did not quite come to that for the present. Nevertheless, Drake had a feeling that it might do so eventually. There was no room for such hostility in such a confined space and he anticipated the outcome with some uneasiness.

Later Schmidt did some more moaning about his thirst, and Bjornssen taunted him again.

'You nothing but a cry-baby. Why don't you go overboard? Plenty water there. Take a good long drink.'

Schmidt said nothing. He seemed to have decided not to be drawn into any further exchange of insults. He just stared at Bjornssen and there was venom in his eyes. It was the kind of look Drake would not have wished to get from him, because there was evil in it.

Maybe the bosun ought to take care.

Night came and they had sighted no ship. Drake found sleep difficult to come by; there was no comfort on the raft, and the motion did nothing to help matters. Nevertheless, he dozed off at times; and once he was wakened by what might have been a cry, though he could not be certain whether this was real or merely part of a dream he had been having.

There was no moon, and in the darkness he could only faintly discern vague shapes that merged with the outlines of the raft. There was no sound now apart from the gentle lapping of water, and he came to the conclusion that there had in fact been no cry except in the hallucination of a dream. He dropped off to sleep again, and the next time he awoke daylight was beginning to reveal the substance of the raft and the men who were on it.

It was then that he realized with a shock that what he had convinced himself was nothing but the ending of a dream had in fact been reality. For when he counted the number of survivors on that tiny floating platform there was no way he could make the total add up to more than three.

CHAPTER TWENTY-FOUR

WATER, WATER, EVERYWHERE

He saw that Gray was still asleep. He saw that the third man was awake and watching him. He saw that it was Hans Schmidt. He woke Gray.

'Bjornssen's gone,' he said.

Gray sat up; wide awake in a moment. 'Gone! How'd it happen?'

Drake pointed at Schmidt.

'Better ask him.'

Gray looked at the German. 'You got anything to say?'

Schmidt shrugged. 'How would I know?'

'I heard a cry in the night,' Drake said. 'I thought at first it was this that awoke me. Then I came to the conclusion that it was just a dream, and I went to sleep again. Now I'm not so sure. Maybe it was Bjornssen crying out.'

Gray looked at Schmidt again. 'You still got nothing to say?'

'Maybe he fall overboard.'

'You don't think maybe he was helped on his way?'

'You accusing me?' Schmidt said.

Gray said nothing.

Drake saw in the increasing light what

appeared to be a stain on some of the slats. He pointed at it.

'That looks like dried blood.' He glanced again at Schmidt. 'Would you say it is?'

'So maybe he had a nose bleed.'

'Just before he fell overboard?'

'Could be.'

Schmidt was lying. That was obvious. Drake felt sure that if the knife in the pigskin sheath on Schmidt's belt had been examined, bloodstains would have been found on it too. Unless he had washed it in the sea. He did not doubt that Schmidt had killed Bjornssen and pushed him overboard. Perhaps they had had another argument and it had come to blows. Or perhaps Schmidt had stuck the knife in just for spite.

But there was no proof.

Gray said: 'You still saying you didn't give him a hand to get himself overboard? Maybe with a knife in the back?'

'Why would I do that?'

'Oh, it may have occurred to you that the provisions would last a bit longer if they were shared between three rather than four.'

'Now that is a thought,' Schmidt said. And he gave a grin.

Drake reflected that if there was more for three than four there would be even more for two, or even one. And if the number on the raft were to be reduced to one he could guess who that survivor would be, according to

Schmidt's way of thinking. He glanced at Gray, and he guessed that this unpleasant possibility had occurred to him also.

But when he spoke it was simply to remark that during the war a Chinese seaman from a sunken British ship had survived for one hundred and forty days alone on a raft in the Atlantic.

'I don't believe it,' Schmidt said.

'You don't have to. But it's fact all the same.'

'What in hell did he live on?'

'Rainwater and flying fish.'

'You reckon we could do that?'

'I hope it won't be necessary,' Gray said.

*　　　*　　　*

There was a brief shower of rain shortly before nightfall, but with only the enamel mug with which to catch the water they were able to make little use of it. And then the cloud that had brought the rain moved away, and night came and the stars glittered.

Drake tried not to sleep, because he did not trust Schmidt. But now, just when he was doing his utmost to avoid closing his eyes, the lids felt as heavy as lead and sleep forced itself on him unbidden.

He awoke suddenly, and there was a sliver of moon casting a silvery radiance on the sea. He could make out the hunched shape of

165

Schmidt facing away from him, and the shape was not moving. So perhaps Schmidt himself had been overcome by the god of sleep and presented no threat to either of those with whom he was sharing the limited accommodation of the raft.

Soon Drake had dozed off again and was dreaming of things quite unconnected with the present situation when he was brought abruptly back to consciousness and the realisation that someone was bending over him.

It was the voice that told him it was Schmidt.

Schmidt was speaking softly; but this softness gave no encouragement for Drake to imagine that his life was not in deadly danger. Schmidt had one hand on his right shoulder, holding him down; and in the other hand, which was raised, the moonlight gleamed on six inches of bare steel, tapering to a point.

Schmidt said: 'I come to say goodbye. You go now to join that gottam Swede. Him last night and you tonight. Then maybe Mister Gray. Two Brits gone and me the sole survivor. The German. How you like that?'

'You're mad,' Drake said. 'You're out of your mind.'

And maybe it was so. Maybe Schmidt really was a nutter. But it did not alter the situation, which was just about as bad as it could be for him, Edgar Drake.

He knew when Schmidt had decided to stop the talking and finish the job, because that right hand of his, the one that was gripping the knife, moved a little higher to make the thrust more effective. There was a fleeting moment then when hand and knife were motionless. Then Schmidt gave a grunt, and Drake saw the blade coming at him. It was aimed at his face, but in the instant before it could reach him he jerked his head to one side and the point just nicked his ear and imbedded itself in the timber beneath him.

Schmidt gave a kind of snarl and hauled the knife out of the woodwork. He was still holding Drake down with his left hand, and he raised his right arm for a second thrust.

But then somebody laughed. And it was not Schmidt and it was not Drake.

Gray laughed and said: 'This for you, Smitty.'

Drake looked past Schmidt and caught a shadowy glimpse of Gray with the hatchet in his hand; the hatchet coming down, the spike leading. There was a sound curiously like the cracking of an eggshell, magnified several times. It was caused by the spike breaking through the top of Schmidt's skull and penetrating the brain.

A thought flashed through Drake's mind; a question: Why the spike and not the blade? But it was irrelevant; either one would have been as effective as the other; and it was

Gray's choice.

'You all right, old boy?' Gray asked.

'Sure,' Drake said.

He got himself free from the encumbrance of Schmidt's dead body; and he was shivering with the reaction. It had been a close thing. It had been too damned close for comfort. 'You took your time.'

Gray laughed again. 'In the nick, old boy, in the nick.'

He sounded exhilarated, as if the killing had given him a kick, set the adrenalin flowing. 'Better get rid of the carcase now.'

Together they rolled Schmidt overboard with the hatchet still imbedded in his skull. He seemed to go straight down. One moment he was there, the next he had gone.

'On our own again,' Gray said. 'Best this way. We should never have let those two bastards come on board. I knew it was a mistake at the time, but you would have it your way. And it nearly did for you.'

Drake said nothing. His ear was bleeding slightly, and he dabbed at it with a handkerchief. It was a mere scratch, but it could have been so much more. He had been close to death, and it was not a pleasant experience.

*   *   *

Dawn came like a punctual guest, dead on

time. There were a few thin wisps of cloud, but the sun was soon hot. There was very little bread or water left now. It was not the hunger that bothered them so much; it was the thirst. It occurred to Drake that the sea had been designed for the express purpose of tormenting shipwrecked sailors. It had all the appearance of an abundance of thirst-quenching liquid surrounding them, and yet it was undrinkable.

'Water, water, everywhere, Nor any drop to drink.' That was what Coleridge had written in 'The Rime of the Ancient Mariner'.

Drake mentioned this to Gray; but it did not go down very well. Gray said he was more concerned with the fate of two young mariners than with that of any number of ancient ones.

'So stuff *Coleridge* and stuff his old seaman too.'

*   *   *

Still they caught no sign of any ship. It was as if this particular area of the Caribbean Sea which they now occupied had been shunned by all vessels, and that in consequence they were condemned to follow those other former crewmen of the *Cronus* into that world from which no traveller had ever returned to tell the tale.

'I refuse to believe it,' Gray said. 'We're too young to die.'

'No one was ever too young for that,' Drake said. 'There's no lower age limit.'

*   *   *

So another day passed, and night came. And the night passed also. And with the morning there came the ship. 'I knew it,' Gray said. 'I told you.'

'So you were right,' Drake said. 'Bully for you, Howard.'

'And bully for you too, Eddie.'

Bully for both of them. No doubt about that.

CHAPTER TWENTY-FIVE

GOLD DUST

Though it was not really a ship. It was a fishing-boat, with sails and an auxiliary engine; an old boat with faded paint and patched sails; a boat that showed no evidence that fishing in those waters was a lucrative occupation.

The members of the crew varied in age; some old, some young. They could have been of one family. They were all dark-skinned and had a weatherbeaten look about them, even the younger ones.

They spoke Spanish with a smattering of

English. Drake and Gray spoke English and a smattering of Spanish. They managed to communicate tolerably well with the aid of sign language.

The rescuers were greatly interested in the raft; they had never seen anything like it. Drake had the impression that they would have liked to take it with them; but it was too big to hoist on board, and towing such an unwieldy craft was out of the question. So, with some reluctance, they had to abandon it. None of them appeared to have noticed the bloodstains on it; and neither Drake nor Gray felt compelled to point them out.

They were given food and drink, and they managed to convey to their rescuers the fact that their ship had sunk in a recent storm and that they were the only survivors.

The language difficulty was something of a blessing in disguise, since it made it impossible to go into details concerning the ship and the manner in which it had come to grief.

*   *   *

The fishing-boat did not return at once to harbour when the rescue had been made. There was still fishing to be done; and to return home with little catch to show apart from two shipwrecked seamen would have been unthinkable. Thus it was several days before Drake and Gray once again sighted

171

land.

*　　　*　　　*

It was a place called Santa Elena, a fishing village situated by a small inlet on the coast of Central America. It did not look a prosperous place; the buildings were mostly adobe, and there were goats and scraggy chickens wandering around, as well as a number of ragged children.

There was an inn of sorts, and the roads were dirt. Dust swirled when the wind blew. Drake and Gray were destined to live there for three weeks. They managed to get a room at the inn, and the people were generally friendly to these two survivors of a tragedy at sea. They knew something of such things from bitter experience. There were widows whose husbands had gone to sea and never returned.

The two Englishmen soon became a feature of the village, and kids followed them around. They earned a little money doing odd jobs, though there were not many of these to be had. Sometimes they helped out on one or other of the fishing-boats. They would have liked to be taken on by some ocean-going ship, but none of these ever entered the tiny harbour of Santa Elena. It was said that there was a port of some importance further along the coast, but there was a certain vagueness concerning the actual size of this port or how far away it was. Drake wondered whether in fact it existed at all and was not some kind of never-never land that no one in the village had actually seen.

They were becoming desperate to get away, but not sure quite how to do it, when Zeke Butler walked into the village with his donkey and a bag of gold dust.

*   *   *

Butler was a little scraggy man, aged around sixty but looking older. He had a mat of grey hair that had not been trimmed in months and a beard of the same description. That part of his body which was not concealed by hair or clothing seemed to have not so much skin as hide. He was slightly bow-legged and he was wearing much scuffed boots, faded blue jeans, an open-necked shirt and a denim jacket. On top of the untrimmed hair he had an ancient Stetson hat with a brim that looked as if mice had been at it.

The donkey was carrying quite a load, including a pick and a spade. In common with most of its kind it had that air of a much abused, much put-upon, but patient animal, resigned to its lot.

Drake and Gray saw man and beast arrive, and their interest was immediately aroused.

'Well now,' Gray said. 'What have we here?'

The kids seemed to know the newcomer,

173

and they crowded round and accompanied him as he made his way to the inn. Drake and Gray, having nothing better to do, went along also.

The man tied his donkey to a rail outside the inn and went inside. The kids stayed outside, but Drake and Gray followed the man.

At that hour of the day not much business was being done by the innkeeper. In fact the bar, a small room with a sanded floor and a ceiling so low that anyone over six feet in height would have had to stoop while moving around in it, was deserted when the newcomer, followed by the two Englishmen, walked into it. There were some rickety chairs and a couple of small tables; while a bar counter at one end had some shelves behind it, on which a very limited variety of bottles was on display.

There was no one behind the bar; but when the grey-haired man rapped on it with his knuckles and also gave a shout the innkeeper appeared from somewhere like a fat, greasy jack-in-the-box.

It was apparent that he recognized the man, for he greeted him in his execrable English.

'Ah, Señor Budler. So you come back, ees not? How pleeze I am to see you. Eez so long time. You okay, no?'

'Sure, sure,' the grey-haired man said. 'Got a thirst though. You got some beer?'

'Sí, sí.'

While the landlord went to fetch the beer, the other man turned to Drake and Gray. He gave them a shrewd look.

'What's a pair like you doing in this neck of the woods? You American?'

'No,' Gray said. 'English.'

'Figures. But what you doing here? This ain't no pleasure resort.'

'You're telling us. Fact is we were on a ship that was wrecked on a reef and sank. We were on a raft for a few days. Ran out of food and water. Got picked up by a fishing-boat and brought here.'

'That a fact? Any other survivors?'

'None.'

'So what you aimin' to do now?'

'That's the problem. We're seamen. We need to be taken on by another ship; but ships don't put in here.'

The landlord came back with a jug of beer and poured out a glass for the grey-haired man, who pointed at Drake and Gray. 'Them too.'

While the landlord poured the drinks the other man introduced himself.

'Ezekiel Butler. Zeke for short. American.'

'I'm Howard Gray. This is Edgar Drake.'

'Shake,' Butler said; and extended a horny hand.

It soon became evident that he liked to talk, mostly about himself. It was a long time since he had had anyone to talk to; and only the

175

donkey for company.

'Which,' he said, 'ain't the best of conversationalists.'

So now, with an audience of two and beer to loosen his tongue, he let the talk flow. And Drake had to admit to himself that it was interesting stuff. It emerged that Zeke Butler was one of a breed that had almost died out: he was a lone prospector. With him the search for gold had been a lifelong passion; and he had carried that search to a number of different countries: Australia, Africa, Central America, and his own native United States.

'Is it much of a living?' Gray asked.

'I get by.'

'Ever strike it rich?'

Butler's eyes seemed to twinkle, as if in reminiscence. 'Once.'

'So what happened?'

'Hit the high life for a time. Riotous living. Dames, gee-gees, gambling, booze; you name it. Blued the lot in six months. Then back to the pick and shovel.'

'Was it worth it?'

Butler's eyes sparkled again, remembering. 'Oh, sure.'

He kept ordering beer for them, and then spirits; but Drake noticed that he never paid a cent. Which seemed odd. Was his credit that good?

It was he himself who explained it. 'Got me a poke of gold dust. Gotta go into town to cash it in. Can't do it here. No bank. You boys wanna see what that stuff looks like?'

They said they did, and he went outside, perhaps a shade unsteady on his feet, and came back with a small leather bag, tied at the top. He untied the bag and showed the contents to them. The stuff inside might have been fine sand, except that sand would never have had that kind of glitter.

Gray said: 'You left this outside on the donkey?'

'Why not? He wouldn't run away with it.'

'Somebody else might.'

'They wouldn't. Guys in this place, they're honest. Poor for sure, but not thieves.'

'Well,' Gray said, 'we'll have to take your word for that. How much is this lot worth?'

Butler grinned. 'A few dollars.'

'Are you going back for more where you got that?' Drake asked.

'Could be. See how I feel.'

A thought had come into Drake's head. He glanced at Gray, and their eyes met, and he guessed that Gray was thinking along the same lines. But it was too early yet. No point in rushing things.

'When you planning to take this to the bank?' Gray asked.

'Maybe tomorrow,' Butler said.

'Want a bodyguard?'

Butler gave a tug at his beard and stared at Gray. 'You looking for a job?'

'We're not all that busy right now,' Gray said.

'I'll have to think about it,' Butler said.

CHAPTER TWENTY-SIX

QUITE A DAY

They went to town the next day with the bag of gold dust; the three of them: Butler, Drake and Gray. Butler seemed to have taken an instant liking to them. Perhaps he was sick of his own company and glad to have someone to talk to.

The town was about twenty-five kilometres inland. It was called San Antonio, and it was where the fishermen of Santa Elena took the fish when they had a good catch. The surplus produce from the small plots of farmland outside the village was also sent there.

There were no taxis or private cars in the village; nor was there any bus service. So they travelled in a Ford pick-up truck that had seen better days. Butler, who was paying the fare, shared the cab with the driver, a young man named Carlos Gamboa, while Drake and Gray rode on the back with a load of vegetable produce and a strong odour of fish. It was a hot day, and dust rose in a cloud from the road behind them. The truck appeared to have lost its silencer, and the engine made a sound like a racing car; which was rather above its station.

The best that could be said for San Antonio, Drake thought, was that it was not Santa Elena. It was certainly bigger. There was a church built in the Spanish colonial style, with white walls and gilding and a bell-tower in which the bell was visible from the outside. There was an open-air market, which had all manner of things for sale and looked pretty busy. And there was, of course, a bank.

They went with Butler to turn his gold dust into cash; and the bank looked to Drake much like those you saw in Western films. But a bank was a bank, whatever it might look like; and a teller with sleek black hair and a black moustache took Butler's gold dust and weighed it without so much as a lifted eyebrow. And then he consulted a set of figures which probably listed the current price of gold on the bullion market, and paid Butler in American dollars, as he had requested.

'Now,' Butler said, 'let's get ourselves a meal.'

*   *   *

It was the best meal Drake could remember having had for quite a while. But of course he had not been feeding in hotels or restaurants in recent times; and wine had not been served with the food even on board the ill-fated S.S.

Cronus. At least not to the deckhands.

After that they took a stroll round the town before finding a bar to prop up. And when Butler had downed a few more drinks he said:

'I'm going to leave you boys for a while. And I want you to look after the dollars, because the place I'm going to it ain't wise to carry too much cash around with you. You get me?'

'You mean you're going to a whorehouse,' Gray said.

Butler gave a wink. 'I know a place.'

'You're too old for that.'

'Hell, no.'

'So what about us?'

'Like I said, you gotta look after the money-bag.'

'Suppose we were to run off with it?'

'Oh, you won't do that. Fact is, I trust you boys.'

*   *   *

When Butler rejoined them it was late in the afternoon, and he suggested they should all go for a drink. So they found another bar, and it emerged that Butler's idea of a drink was in the plural rather than the singular. By the time they left the bar, therefore, they were having to support their companion, whose legs appeared to be no longer under the control of their owner.

180

Then they discovered that the pick-up truck was not at the place where they had agreed to rejoin it for the return journey to Santa Elena.

'The bastard's gone without us,' Gray said. 'Would you believe it?'

Drake found it only too easy to believe, seeing that it was now some three hours past the time they had arranged to be picked up. It was apparent that, not unnaturally, the driver had become fed up with waiting for his passengers, and had decided to make for home and leave them to return to the village as best they could.

'So what do we do now?' Gray said. 'It'd be a long walk.' It was Butler who suggested a taxi.

'If we can find one to take us that far,' Drake said. Which he thought was doubtful.

*   *   *

It took some time to find one, but they succeeded eventually. The taxi looked as if it had seen its best days a long time ago. And the driver looked like a brigand. He also acted like a brigand in demanding an exorbitant fare, to be paid in advance.

Both Drake and Gray thought this was an unreasonable demand; but Butler, with money in his pocket, was in a profligate mood and made no bones about agreeing to the figure. He would also have been prepared to hand

181

over the full amount at once; but his younger companions persuaded him not to do this. They feared that the driver, with the fare safely extracted, would be likely to dump his passengers a short distance beyond the limits of the town and leave them stranded many miles from their destination.

The argument continued for some time, during which the prospective customers threatened to find alternative transport, while the driver made a series of the most expressive shrugs of the shoulders that Drake had ever seen. But finally agreement was reached. This was that half the fare, exorbitant as it was, would be paid in advance, and that the other half would be handed over only after the journey had been satisfactorily completed.

So they all got in, with Gray sitting beside the driver and the other two in the back. And before they had gone more than a hundred yards Butler was asleep and snoring.

It was dark now, and it appeared that only one of the taxi's headlights was working. Moreover, this had a disconcerting habit of going out now and then, before coming on again. This did not appear to bother the driver, who was hunched over the wheel and driving like a madman. If the taxi had been capable of going faster no doubt he would have been pleased to make it do so; disregarding the potholes in the road which threatened to cause irreperable damage to the vehicle's suspension.

Drake was not altogether surprised when the engine broke down; it had appeared inevitable. He supposed one had to feel fortunate that this mishap occurred when they were no more than a kilometre or so from their destination.

He woke Butler and they all got out. The driver, in a fit of rage, kicked the nearside front wheel of the taxi and injured his toe. He was even more enraged when Gray told him that, since his side of the verbal contract had not been completed, he would not be getting the remaining half of the fare. Gray said this in English, but the man seemed to get the gist of the statement; whereupon he protested vehemently, with much gesticulation of the hands and stamping of the feet.

Butler might have been again inclined to give way and pay up. He was still in a generous mood, though only half awake. But Gray, with the support of Drake, refused to let him be conned by this rogue of a taxi driver, whose vehicle had been demonstrably unequal to the service required of it.

In the end they simply walked away and left the man to shout abuse at them until they were out of earshot.

Not that the walking away was quite as simple as it might have been, since Butler's legs were still not in proper working order and the two younger men were forced to support him, one on either side. They even had to carry him whenever he fell asleep, which he did far too often for their comfort.

Nevertheless, he came fully awake when they reached the inn at Santa Elena, and immediately ordered drinks for all those who happened to be there; which, fortunately for the state of his purse, was not a great number.

Eventually he fell asleep again and could not be wakened. So Drake and Gray carried him to his room and put him to bed.

'Been quite a day,' Gray said. 'All things considered.'

Drake saw no reason to disagree with that verdict.

CHAPTER TWENTY-SEVEN

BORING JOB

'We've got a proposal to put to you, Zeke,' Gray said.

It was the morning after the visit to San Antonio, and they were sitting in the inn in Santa Elena.

Butler was not looking well. It was obvious that he was suffering from a hangover, and it was possibly not the best of times for putting a proposition to him. But Drake and Gray had talked the matter over and had decided that there was little point in postponing it.

Butler looked at Gray with a somewhat watery eye; maybe a trifle suspiciously.

'You have?'

'Yes.'

'So let's have it, son. Spit it out.'

But Gray answered with a question: 'When are you planning to leave here?'

'What's it to you?'

'A matter of interest.'

'Well, as a matter of interest, I aim to leave here when I damn please.'

'Which will be when the money runs out. Right?'

'Maybe.'

'You going to try your luck again?'

'Could be.'

'Well, it's like this. Eddie and I thought, you being not quite as young as you used to be, might like a bit of help.'

Suddenly Butler gave a cackling laugh.

'Ah, now I get you. What you're proposing is that you two young heroes come along with me. Am I right?'

'You're right,' Gray said.

'You wouldn't like it.'

'Why not?'

'It's tough going.'

'We're tough,' Gray said. 'We're seamen. We've been around. Worked hard.'

'Servin' in ships ain't like pannin' for gold. Offhand I can't think of two more different

185

occupations.'

'Look,' Drake said, 'we know we'd have to learn the business, but you can show us how it's done.'

'You thinkin 'bout gettin rich quick, forget it,' Butler said.

'Me, I been at it more'n half my life, and you think I look rich?'

'You brought in a bag of gold dust the other day.'

'And worked mighty hard to get it.'

'So the answer is no?'

'Now don't start jumpin' to conclusions. Let's chew this over some.'

He took a bitten-down pipe from his pocket, loaded it with some dark tobacco, tamped it down and lit it with a match. When he had it going to his satisfaction he said:

'You serious about this?'

'You bet your life we are,' Gray said. 'And what's more, I think we'd make a good team.'

It took them the best part of two hours to convince Butler of this; but Drake had a feeling that he had had a liking for the idea right from the start. Maybe he was a bit tired of the solitary life.

'Did you ever have a partner before?' Drake asked.

Butler nodded. 'Once. He turned out to be a real low-down sonuvabitch. Did the dirty on me and hightailed it with my share as well as his.'

186

'We wouldn't do that,' Gray said. 'I give you my word.'

'For what it's worth,' Butler said.

And sucked at his pipe.

*   *   *

They set out a week later. Drake and Gray had rucksacks which they had picked up in San Antonio, along with certain other items of equipment that Butler had said might prove useful. The main part of the load was carried by the patient donkey. Butler, by reason of his age, travelled light.

Their departure aroused a little interest in the village, and a pack of children accompanied them for a short distance before losing the urge and returning home. They were then on their own, heading in a westerly direction, but not on the road that led to San Antonio. When Drake had inquired where Butler was leading them he had been answered briefly.

'The sierra.'

Which was vague, to say the least, but was all the detail the old man seemed prepared to give. He had no map, but he had a pocket compass, which he consulted occasionally.

*   *   *

They travelled some twenty-five miles on the

first day. To Drake and Gray, sweating under the weight of their rucksacks, it seemed at least twice the distance. The dirt road gradually deteriorated into little better than a rough track; and they met no one. They made camp in a hollow where a few stunted trees were growing, and next day they moved on.

'How much farther is it?' Gray asked.

'Quite a way,' Butler said. He gave a slightly sardonic grin. 'Now don't tell me you're tired already.'

'I think I may have blisters on the feet,' Gray said.

'Well, you said you could do it. If you boys want to pull out now you can head back home as soon as you please. And I'll go on by myself.'

'Are you kidding?' Gray said. 'We'd be pretty damn crazy to do that, wouldn't we? I was just asking a question.'

'Well,' Butler said, 'I can tell you this much. It won't be tomorrow, nor yet the next day. But if we keep goin' we'll get there eventually.'

He still had not told them precisely where 'there' was. Perhaps, Drake thought, he did not know himself. It might be the place where he had got his last bag of gold dust, or he might be planning to try his luck somewhere else. They would just have to wait and see. Zeke Butler could be pretty much of a clam when it suited him.

*　　*　　*

It took them almost a week to reach their destination after a journey that had taken them across some pretty rough terrain: scrub, tufty grass, rock. This part of the country appeared to be completely uninhabited; it was probably just too poor for farming, or even the grazing of cattle. After a time they had the sierra in sight, but Butler said it was farther away than it seemed. The ground became ever more rocky as they drew nearer to the foothills; and then one day, without any warning from their guide, they were at journey's end.

It was a surprise to Drake. There were some buildings of a sort: dilapidated wooden huts, with no sign that anyone was living in them or had been doing so for a long time. There were some bits and pieces of machinery, quietly rusting away, a garbage dump, nothing new. From a source somewhere higher up a stream of clear water ran down.

'What's this?' Drake said.

Butler shook his head. 'That's the wrong question. You should have asked what it was.'

'So what was it?'

'A gold mine.'

Drake stared at him. 'Are you serious?'

'Too right, I am. Years gone by this would have been a busy place, I guess. Though I never saw it then.'

'So why's it been abandoned?' Gray said.

'The best of reasons. The gold ran out.'

'Then why've you brought us here? I thought the idea was to go where there is gold, not where there used to be.'

'Now hold your hosses,' Butler said. 'This was a big operation, so there'd need to be enough of the yellow stuff to make it worth the investment. For a time there must've been; but I guess it was a wasting asset. Time came when the amount extracted didn't pay the expense of getting it. So they closed down the operation and made tracks. Don't mean all the gold's been took. Where d'you think I got the sack of dust I brought to Santa Elena? Right here, son. And where I got that we can get more. Won't make us rich, but that's the way it is.'

'How do we do it?' Drake asked.

'We pan for it, that's what. See the creek there?'

'Yes.'

'See the way it widens out and gets shallow? That's where the gold is, in them beds of gravel. The water brings it down from the hills and it gets deposited there. That's where I got my last lot, and that's where we're going to get more. You ever done any panning for gold?'

Drake shook his head. 'Never. We told you.'

'So I'll have to teach you. With the three of us going at it we should get a useful little pile before long. But you gotta have patience.'

He was right about that. After two or three days of it Drake came to the conclusion that he had never had a more boring job; or one that made his back ache so much.

Panning was simple enough when you got the hang of it. You scooped up some gravel from the bed of the stream where the shallows were, and then by a careful motion of the pan you washed away the lighter sand and shingle until there was just the heavier gold dust left behind. Then you did it again. And again. And again.

It was a slow process, and Drake could see that it was no way of making a quick fortune. He could also see that Gray was getting sick of it even more rapidly than he was. And not making much effort to disguise the fact.

It had of course been the arrival of Zeke Butler in the village with his bag of gold dust that had caught their imagination. They had seen the result but had not given a thought to the long weeks of monotonous and lonely toil that had had to be endured in order to accumulate such an amount. Now they knew what was entailed, and they were not liking it at all.

*　　*　　*

Some days it rained, and they spent the time in

one of the huts, which still had a roof that leaked only in places. They played cards, and Butler smoked his pipe, and time dragged.

They were hardly living on the fat of the land either. Bacon and beans; beans and bacon; hard biscuit in lieu of bread; black coffee to drink.

'Is this what you've been doing all your life, Zeke?' Gray asked.

'Not all my life,' Butler said. 'I was a boy once.'

'You don't say.'

'What's eating you, son? Can't you take it? As I recall, it was you begged me to to take you along. I didn't ask you to come.'

'We must have been crazy.'

'Not crazy, I guess. Just greedy. You smelt easy money and thought you'd like a fistful. Now you find you have to work for it, you ain't so happy.'

'No,' Gray said, 'I'm not so happy. When do you think we'll have enough of the stuff for us to up stakes and head back to Santa Elena?'

'Well now, that depends on how much you want. We could go tomorrow, but it would hardly have been worth the journey.'

'How about giving it another week?' Drake suggested.

Rather to his surprise, Butler immediately agreed to this. He would have been more surprised, however, if he had not had a suspicion that the old-man's health was not nearly as good as he had always tried to give the impression that it was. Drake wondered whether his heart was giving him some trouble. On one or two occasions he had seen him appear to lose his breath; and sometimes he would stop working to go and sit down for a while. He might simply have been taking a rest because he was feeling tired; but Drake suspected that there was more to it than this.

Anyway, for whatever reason, Butler seemed agreeable to the termination of their stay at the old mine workings; and though they had no great quantity of gold dust to show for their labours, it was at least something. And they had had an interesting experience.

None of them had an inkling then of the manner in which the outlook for all of them was to be so completely transformed three days later. And indeed, unless they had been endowed with the gift of second sight, there was no way they could have had.

And, as Drake remarked later, it was not just one chance in a million; it was one in a thousand million. And maybe more than that.

CHAPTER TWENTY-EIGHT

THE STONE

Just five days before they were due to pull up stakes and leave the old mine workings Butler had what he himself described as a nasty turn.

Drake thought that this was a mild way of putting it. His own guess was that the old man had had a slight heart attack; though this could be no more than a guess. What was certain, however, was that Butler had collapsed while working and had blacked out. It had taken them some time to revive him, and he was persuaded to take a rest for the remainder of the day.

He did this only reluctantly; he seemed unwilling to admit that there could be anything seriously wrong with him; and the next day he resumed work as usual.

Thus it was that he was present when Drake made the find that was to make such a change in their fortunes.

It was in a batch of gravel he had lifted from the bed of the stream. It looked like a stone of irregular shape, and it was bigger than any of the pebbles around it. It was light brown in colour, and there was a glassy look about it, but no sparkle. His immediate inclination was to throw it away; but there was something

194

about the object that made him hesitate. Instead, he walked over to where Butler was working and showed it to him. 'You ever seen a stone like this?'

Butler took it from him, rubbed the smooth surface with his fingers, and held it up to let the sunlight fall on it. He turned it over in his hands, examining it from every angle; and Drake could sense the growing excitement in him. Suddenly he let out a yell.

'Yippee!'

Gray, attracted by the shout, walked over to see what it was about.

'You gone crazy, Zeke?'

'Betcha life, I have,' Butler said. And he did a little dance, holding the stone aloft. 'Boys, we've hit the jackpot. You know what this is?'

'Looks like a stone to me,' Gray said.

'And so it is. But not just any old stone. This here is a diamond. A genuine diamond. We've made it, boys, we've made it. We're in the money.'

'Now I know you're crazy. You're off your nut. I mean to say, does it look like a diamond?'

'You think it don't?'

'Dead right in one.'

'Well, let me ask you a question. Have you ever seen a rough diamond? One that's never been cut?'

Gray had to admit that he had not.

'Have you?'

'Sure, I have. Time back I was in South Africa. Went to the diamond mines. Saw the whole shebang. Had an overseer's job for a coupla years before movin' on. So don't tell me I don't know what a diamond looks like in the raw.'

Drake said: 'Are you telling the truth? You're not just kidding us, are you?'

'No, I ain't just kiddin'. This is the real McCoy.'

'But the size of it. Did you ever see one as big as this?'

'No. But I've seen some pretty big ones.'

'That was a long time ago,' Gray said. He was still not buying it. 'Maybe your memory's not so good.'

Drake was doubtful too; but he could see that Butler was completely serious on this score. And if he had worked in the South African diamond industry he would surely know what he was talking about.

'So if you're right. If this really is a diamond, what's it worth? Roughly.'

Butler fingered the stone, turning it over and over, examining it from every angle. It seemed to fascinate him.

'Stone like this, it'd go to the cutters in Antwerp or Amsterdam maybe. It'd be cut so's there'd be one big one and some smaller ones. It's the cutting makes it come to life. The big one, oh my, she'd really be worth the shekels.'

'But this one here, just the way it is, if we

were to sell it?'

Butler pursed his lips and made a low hissing sound. 'Boys, we're not talking thousands, not tens or hundreds of thousands. We're talking millions. We're talking each one of us a millionaire.'

Gray, in spite of himself, seemed to be impressed. 'Millionaires, huh? Well, that beats working hours on end for a few grains of gold dust. It really does.'

'Sure. But if we hadn't been looking for gold we'd never have found this.'

It occurred to Drake that he was the one who had found it; not Gray nor Butler. But of course they had been working as a team, so he was not going to make a point of this. Each of them was entitled to an equal share. And if Butler was right one third of the total would be plenty.

There remained the little matter of selling it.

'Who would be in the market for one big rough diamond?'

'Oh,' Butler said, 'that's easy. In practice there's just one buyer, and that's De Beers. They have pretty well a monopoly.'

'And they would give us a fair price?'

'I guess so.'

It was enough to make the head swim. One minute you're breaking your back to get a few dollars' worth of pay-dirt; the next you've got a fortune in your hand. You're made for life.

'I guess you boys are glad now I brung you along with me,' Butler said.

'Right in one,' Gray said. 'And aren't you glad we came?'

Butler grinned. 'Well, you never know. Maybe I'd have found it for myself.'

'And maybe you wouldn't. It could have stayed where it was for ever. Nobody knowing. Nobody even suspecting. Aren't we just the lucky ones?'

*   *   *

They decided to leave the next day. There was hardly much point in continuing to pan for a few more grains of gold when they had a fortune in their hands. The sooner they got the diamond to the buyer, the better. And they had a long journey ahead of them.

A question occurred to Drake. 'How do we get in touch with De Beers?'

'I been thinking about that,' Butler said. 'I guess we could send a cable from San Antonio. Or put a phone call through to their London or New York office. It's no great problem.'

'Wouldn't they think it was just a hoax?'

'They might. But they'd be bound to check. They might send a man out. Don't worry. It'll all come right. You'll see.'

There was a problem nevertheless. And the problem was Zeke Butler himself. It became apparent on the very first day of their journey that he was not going to find it easy to make the grade. His breathing was laboured, and it was obvious that, even without a pack, his pace of walking was never going to match that which he had kept up on the outward journey.

In answer to any inquiries concerning his health he would answer somewhat tetchily that he was all right.

'Out of practice, that's all. Another day or two I'll be OK. Don't worry about me.'

But they had to worry. On the first day they covered less than half the distance they were managing before; and it was only too apparent that, despite his protestations, Butler was not a fit man. When they made camp he let the younger men do the work, while he sat down and smoked his pipe.

On the second day they covered even less distance than they had on the first. When they made camp Gray took Drake aside and said: 'What are we going to do about the old man?'

'What can we do? We'll just have to go at his pace.'

'Frankly, I don't think the old bastard will make it.'

'Oh, it's not as bad as that,' Drake said. But he too had his doubts.

'It's going to take a hell of a long time to reach Santa Elena at this pace.'

'So what if it does? A few more days aren't going to make all that difference.'

'Damned nuisance all the same.'

'For him I'd say it's a lot more than a nuisance,' Drake said.

It seemed to him that Gray was thinking only of himself. But that was nothing new. Had he not once said he believed in looking after number one? And number one was Howard Gray, not Ezekiel Butler.

What Gray was eager for now was getting his hands on the money that the diamond was going to bring him. He just could not bear the thought of having to travel at Butler's pace. But he would just have to resign himself to it, because there was no way he, Drake, was going to hurry the old man, even if that were possible.

* * *

It rained on the fourth day, briefly but heavily; and they all got wet. Gray cursed the weather, and was morose for the rest of the day and the evening.

'What's eating you, son?' Butler asked.

Gray turned on him. 'You know damn well what's eating me. It's the snail's pace we're going at. How long is it going to take us at this rate?'

'A few more days, I guess. What's your hurry? Can't wait to get your hands on the dough? You're too impatient.'

'Well, aren't you?'

'Oh, sure I am. And I got more reason to

200

be. I ain't as young as you. Don't have so many years ahead of me to enjoy the high life. But I can wait a bit longer. Patience, boy, that's what you need. Patience.'

Gray turned away, and Drake could see that he was close to losing his temper. He was in no mood to take a lecture from Zeke Butler on the subject of patience. It never had been one of his virtues.

*   *   *

Next morning Butler's health had taken a turn for the worse. Drake guessed that he had had a bad night; though he did not admit as much. All he said was that he was not feeling quite up to scratch and thought it best if they had a rest for the day.

'You mean we're to hang around here for another twenty-four hours?' Gray made no attempt to hide his disgust. 'What are we supposed to do? Just hang around twiddling our thumbs?'

Butler answered tartly, though in a somewhat weaker voice than was normal with him: 'What you do with your thumbs is your business. And if you don't want to stay, there's nothing to prevent you going on ahead.' He turned to Drake. 'How about you? You in a hurry to get going as well?'

'No,' Drake said. 'I'll stay with you as long as it takes. Maybe tomorrow you'll be feeling better. Hell, what's a day or two more or less? It's the years ahead that count.'

Gray turned his back on them and walked away. But Drake felt pretty sure he would not be leaving on his own. He would not wish to put a distance between himself and the diamond.

In one sense he was entirely correct; but in another he could not have been more wrong.

CHAPTER TWENTY-NINE

SKUNK

Drake woke in the morning with a feeling that something was wrong. It was odd, but it was there; a kind of sixth sense.

It was not yet fully light. There were a few stunted trees and some bushes on the rim of the hollow where they had made camp, and they were not yet clearly defined. He could see the donkey standing quite motionless, and not far from it the dark shape on the ground that he knew was Butler in his sleeping-bag.

But there was something wrong, and a moment later he knew what it was. Between him and Butler there should have been another sleeper; and there was not. The space was empty; the space where Gray should have been.

He was out of his sleeping-bag in a moment. He was out of it and checking up; hoping he was wrong, but all too sure that he was not.

He woke Butler.

'Howard's gone.'

Butler sat up. 'Gone? You sure?'

'His kit's not here.'

'So he decided to go on ahead after all. But why in the night? Without telling us.' And then, as a thought seemed to come to him: 'He wouldn't.'

'If you're thinking what I'm thinking, my guess is he would. Knowing Howard.'

Yet he still could hardly believe it. Surely not even Howard Gray would pull a trick like that.

It took less than a quarter of a minute to prove that he would. And had.

'The low-down, stinking, thieving skunk!' Butler said. The stone had gone.

Drake felt sick.

There had been two small bags of gold dust. Gray had taken one but had left the other.

'Generous of him,' Butler said. 'I guess he figured he'd need one lot for expenses. He'll not be able to cash in on the diamond straightaway.'

'If we could just catch him—'

'You might on your own. You'd have to leave me. Maybe that's what you'd better do. I'm no use to you now.'

'Forget it,' Drake said. 'You're coming with

me.'

*   *   *

They made less than five miles that day; and Butler was struggling. Drake was really worried about him. He looked ill; there was no colour in his face and he seemed to breathe with difficulty. He had given up smoking his pipe.

'For the good of my health,' he said, with a wry grin. 'Bit late in life, but as they say, better late than never.'

That evening he talked quite a lot; recounting incidents in a life that had apparently had plenty of them.

'You ought to write a book,' Drake said.

This seemed to amuse him. 'Story of a Ne'er-Do-Well?'

'It'd make a good story. Might be a bestseller.'

'I'm no writer.'

'Doesn't matter. Get a ghost to do the writing.'

'I never knew ghosts could write.'

'You'd be surprised. Some make a good living at it, so I've been told.'

'Is that a fact?'

'Sure.'

'I'll have to think about it.'

'You do that,' Drake said.

He was not sure when Butler died. It must have been some time during the night, because he was dead when he went to rouse him.

It hit him hard. He had really come to like the old man. Now Gray had taken off with the diamond and Butler was dead. So he was on his own and had to decide what course to take.

The first task was a sad one. He had to dig a grave and bury the dead man. He could not simply leave him to the scavengers.

The ground was stony, and it took him some time. He was sweating when he had finished; and it was not as deep as some he had seen in graveyards. But he was pretty sure Butler would not complain. There was no coffin; but he used the sleeping-bag in place of one; and he dragged the body to the grave and eased it in.

He wondered whether he ought to say a prayer or something of the kind; but he could think of nothing appropriate, and he doubted whether Butler had had much time for religion anyway. So in the end he just said:

'Farewell, old pal. Happy landings.'

Then he started the filling-in; and before long the body in its wrapping had disappeared from sight. He paused then for a while to ease his back, and then went on to complete the job. A little mound of earth and stones marked the grave, and he thought of putting up something in the way of a headstone, maybe with Butler's name and the date. But finally he rejected that idea too.

The donkey presented a problem. He could have taken it along with him, but he doubted whether it would have been wise; so he decided simply to give it its freedom. It had been a slave for a long time; how long he had no idea, since he was no expert regarding the age of this kind of beast of burden. But he had heard that donkeys were more intelligent than horses when it came to the push, and he had no doubt that this one would be able to look after itself with no one to put a load on its back.

He packed some provisions in his rucksack and topped up his canteen of water with what was left in Butler's. He took the compass, which he thought might help him to find his way back to the coast, and was rather surprised that Gray had left it. He took the remaining bag of gold dust and stowed it in his pack, and then he was ready to go.

The donkey followed him for a little way, but it seemed confused; perhaps missing its old master and the load on its back. So after a while it decided to turn around and go back the way it had come. And that was the last Drake saw of it.

* * *

It took him four days to get to the dirt road, and he was fairly pleased with himself for being successful in finding it. He wondered whether Gray had done as well; he had seen no sign of him, and for days he had encountered no other human being. The first person he saw on the road was an old man on a rusty bicycle; and later that day he met a lorry and some other traffic as he approached more closely to the coast.

He decided not to go back to Santa Elena, because if he arrived in the village with a bag of gold and neither of the companions who had departed with him not so long ago it might raise questions which he would find difficult to answer satisfactorily. Therefore, he made a diversion before reaching the village and got himself on to the road that led to San Antonio.

He did not reach the town until the next day; and he wondered whether Gray had been there earlier, or was even there now, since he too would have had good reason not to return to Santa Elena. He kept his eyes open for any sight of the man, but saw no sign of him. It would have surprised him if he had; for Gray, with the diamond in his possession, would be keen to get away from that area as quickly as possible. Drake could only make a guess at what his plans might be, but he had little hope of catching him.

As for himself, the first act was to get the little bag of gold dust changed into cash; and for this purpose he went, not to the bank where Butler had made his exchange, and where there was the faint possibility that he might be recognized, but to a shop that appeared to be a cross between a jeweller's and a pawnbroker's. Here he had no doubt that he was cheated, but there were no questions asked. He was quoted a figure and he accepted it without haggling.

*   *   *

Two days later he was in a port farther south along the coast. A week later he had been taken on as an able seaman on board a Greek cargo ship and was back in the old routine. But no longer with Howard Gray as a shipmate.

CHAPTER THIRTY

FORGET IT

He stayed with the Greek freighter for a year. He stayed with her until the day when she put in to the port of London. He decided then that he had had enough of the seagoing life and wanted no more of it. He signed off, took his pay and walked down the gangplank for the last time with his kit on his shoulder.

A month later he was back with the Apex

Insurance Company at their new London office. They were recruiting staff and were pleased to take him on again. So he slipped back into the fold he had left almost ten years earlier, and soon it was as though he had never been away. The great difference was that he now had no bosom pal in the office named Howard Gray.

He made some inquiries about the man, but nobody seemed to know anything about him. His parents were still in India, but he made no attempt to contact them. They would probably have known less about their son than he did.

So the years passed, and he gained regular promotion and rises in salary. He married one of the girls in the office, and they moved into a small terrace house in Kilburn. When the first child was born, a boy they named Rex, they started looking for somewhere better and found a semi-detached in Edgware. It was there that their second child was born. This was a girl whom they named Wendy.

Later they bought a house in Totteridge with the help of a mortgage; and that was where the children grew up and eventually flew away to make nests of their own. It was all a pretty mundane story, which could not have been more different from those years during and just after the war. Sometimes Pat, Drake's wife, would ask him about that part of his life, but he was reticent concerning it. She had never known Howard Gray, having joined the company after his departure; so she had no idea of what a charmer he had been. And what a skunk.

*   *   *

When Drake retired he and Pat, with son and daughter off their hands, planned to enjoy life: travel a bit, potter about in the garden, go to plays . . .

It all came to nothing, because Pat died from a cancer soon after his retirement and he was left on his own. The house in Totteridge was too big for him, and he sold it and moved into a flat. He had been living there for six years when he read the obituary in the *Daily Telegraph.*

*   *   *

So Gray had been living in England for years and he had never known it. And apparently he had been a man of some importance; managing director of a prosperous engineering firm which he himself had built up from scratch. There was no mention in the obituary of his early life, the war years, and just after. It was as if for him everything had started when he founded the company.

And where had the capital for starting that company come from? There was no mention of that either; no mention of the diamond that

Gray must have sold to De Beers. But of course old Howard had no doubt seen to it that there should be no publicity about the deal; and De Beers might have been willing enough to keep it confidential if the seller wished it to be.

He wondered when Gray had returned to England. Maybe when he himself had been working his guts out on board that filthy Greek freighter, which was owned by a multimillionaire who had started his business career as an ice-cream vendor and spare-time pimp.

He had long since got over the bitterness regarding Gray's treachery, which had robbed him of a fortune; but now it revived. It irked him to reflect that, while he had been plodding his way up the hill of promotion to a not very elevated position in the Apex hierarchy, his erstwhile pal had been rolling in wealth and all that wealth could buy: grand houses, Rolls-Royce cars, a sea-going yacht maybe, and possibly an expensive mistress or two. How old Howard must have revelled in that sort of thing; not giving a damn for those he had cheated out of their rightful share in the wealth. And after all, was it not he, Edgar Drake, who had found the diamond?

*　　　*　　　*

He decided to pay a call on Mrs Gray, the widow. He wondered just how much she knew regarding her late husband's early life. Would he have confided everything in her? Drake much doubted it.

He made some inquiries with the company, and an obliging female gave him the address and telephone number that he required. The place was down in Hertfordshire, and he drove out there and was not surprised when he saw it. It was a country house that proclaimed wealth. A long gravel drive led up to it, and there was a paddock with horses grazing, stabling in the background. The house was old, possibly Georgian, Virginia creeper on the walls, a portico over the front door, tall windows.

There was a Bentley standing on the gravel. It made Drake's old Ford look like a poor relation.

A Filipino maidservant answered the door when he rang the bell; and he gave his name.

'I have an appointment with Mrs Gray.'

She conducted him to a large drawing-room, expensively furnished, and the woman was waiting for him. She was rather younger than he had expected; certainly younger than Howard Gray would have been; attractive in a mature way; dressed in a cashmere jumper and white slacks.

She had been standing by one of the windows when he entered. She turned and looked at him. He had a feeling that he was being weighed in the balance of her mind, and

212

he wondered whether he was making the grade.

'Ah,' she said. 'Mr Drake.' She did not offer to shake hands but indicated a chair. 'Do sit down.'

He did so. It was one of those armchairs which seem to be designed to accommodate at least two people of normal size. Mrs Gray sat on another one, facing him.

'I must confess,' she said, 'that your telephone call took me rather by surprise. Howard never mentioned your name as far as I can recall. But you were a friend of his, you say?'

'Yes. But it was a long time ago. We were both young. We had lost touch latterly.'

He was not surprised that Gray had not spoken of him. He would not have wished to reveal too much concerning his early life. Possibly he had conjured up an entirely fictitious story to cover that period. He wondered whether this woman knew about the diamond. Probably not.

'So you were in the war together?'

'Yes.'

'Well, of course he never spoke much about that. I think he preferred to forget. It must have been rather horrible.'

'It was, at times.'

'It was several years after the war when we met. He was already in business then; building up this company of his.'

'He had some capital, did he? To get it started, I mean.'

'Well, yes, I suppose so.' She seemed a trifle surprised by the question. 'As I understand it, he had come into a legacy of some sort. But he never went into details, and I never inquired. I felt that all that sort of thing was really not my concern.'

Just take the money and don't ask awkward questions, Drake thought. He had the impression that she regarded all such matters as really rather sordid and best ignored.

'And he never mentioned my name?'

She shook her head. 'If he did I must have forgotten. You were close friends at one time, you say?'

'Oh yes. After we left school we worked in the same office. And then the war came and we decided to get in straightaway So we volunteered. We served in the same ships, and a couple of them were sunk under us. And then after the war we worked as seamen for a time. But then we—'

He stopped. He saw that Mrs Gray was staring at him in a very odd sort of way.

'Is anything wrong?' he asked.

'Wrong?' she said. 'Well, of course there is. Are you telling me you were in the Navy during the war?'

'Why, yes. DEMS actually'

'And Howard was with you?'

'For the first part, yes. Until we were both

214

promoted to leading seamen.'

'But this is crazy,' she said. 'My husband was never in the Navy. He was a soldier.'

It was Drake's turn to stare. 'Are you sure?'

'What do you mean, am I sure?' Her voice was like ice, and she was looking at him as if he were something nasty the cat had brought in. 'He was my husband, wasn't he?'

'Yes, of course,' And then it struck him. 'Oh, my God! It's a different Howard Gray. I didn't think. I just took it for granted. I'm so sorry. So awfully sorry. I—'

He was stammering. He felt an absolute idiot. He had jumped to a conclusion, just because of the name and because that picture in the paper had looked uncannily like his Howard Gray grown older. And so he had made this terrible blunder.

'I think,' she said, 'you had better leave now, Mr Drake.'

'Yes,' he said. 'Yes, I will, at once.' He was edging towards the door. 'I do apologize most sincerely. I don't know how I could have been so stupid.'

She seemed to relent a little then. And she even gave a smile, which quite transformed her face.

'Don't let it bother you, Mr Drake. We all make mistakes, don't we? It was good of you to come; even if you got the wrong Howard.'

Somehow he got himself out of the house; somehow he got into his car and drove away from the portico and the Bentley on the gravel and the horses in the paddock. And all the way back to his flat he was cursing himself and wondering just where the real Howard Gray, his Howard, was, and thinking that perhaps now he would never know.

So forget it, Eddie. It's past, done with, finished.

But how could you ever forget a diamond as big as that one he had once held in his hand? Scott Fitzgerald wrote a story called 'The Diamond as Big as the Ritz'. His had not been as big as that; but it had been big, really big. And Howard had stolen it from him.

How could you forget a thing like that?

CHAPTER THIRTY-ONE

SKELETON

A party of young men were pony-trekking in a sparsely inhabited region of Central America when they came upon the skeleton of a man.

It was in a shallow depression, and it had obviously been there for a very long time. Time enough for the clothing to rot away and for the scavengers to take the flesh off the bones. Nearby were the remains of what had apparently been a rucksack; and there was an empty metal canteen. There was also a scattering of what looked like fine sand; and one of the men laughingly said:

'Gold dust.'

But none of them believed that this was what it really was. And even if it had been, how could you have picked it up?

Regarding the skeleton, the only conclusion they could come to was that it was that of a man who had lost his way in that desolate country and had starved to death. What was strange about it was that, still clutched in one bony hand, was a large stone. They prised it from the fingers and examined it closely; but, apart from a certain lustre in parts, they could see nothing unusual about it.

They threw it away and rode on, leaving the skeleton where they had found it.

We hope you have enjoyed this Large Print book. Other Chivers Press or Thorndike Press Large Print books are available at your library or directly from the publishers.

For more information about current and forthcoming titles, please call or write, without obligation, to:

Chivers Large Print
published by BBC Audiobooks Ltd
St James House, The Square
Lower Bristol Road
Bath BA2 3SB
UK
email: bbcaudiobooks@bbc.co.uk
www.bbcaudiobooks.co.uk

OR

Thorndike Press
295 Kennedy Memorial Drive
Waterville
Maine 04901
USA
www.gale.com/thorndike
www.gale.com/wheeler

All our Large Print titles are designed for easy reading, and all our books are made to last.